MAX

SPY F

THE AMAZON EXPERIMENT

MAX REMY SPY FORCE

THE AMAZON EXPERIMENT

D. ABELA

OXFORD
UNIVERSITY PRESS

OXFORD
UNIVERSITY PRESS

Great Clarendon Street, Oxford OX2 6DP

Oxford University Press is a department of the University of Oxford.
It furthers the University's objective of excellence in research,
scholarship, and education by publishing worldwide in

Oxford New York

Auckland Cape Town Dar es Salaam Hong Kong Karachi
Kuala Lumpur Madrid Melbourne Mexico City Nairobi
New Delhi Shanghai Taipei Toronto

With offices in

Argentina Austria Brazil Chile Czech Republic France Greece
Guatemala Hungary Italy Japan Poland Portugal Singapore
South Korea Switzerland Thailand Turkey Ukraine Vietnam

First published 2004 by Random House Australia Pty Ltd

First published in the UK 2006

British Library Cataloguing in Publication Data

Data available

ISBN-13: 978-0-19-275422-6
ISBN-10: 0-19-275422-X

1 3 5 7 9 10 8 6 4 2

Printed in Great Britain by Cox & Wyman Ltd., Reading, Berkshire

For Jack

CHAPTER 1

A MENACING DOWNPOUR AND A REQUEST FROM STEINBERGER

The rain plummeted in sheets as Max scurried through the twisting, cobbled streets of Venice. Water poured from burst downpipes, washed into moored gondolas, and overflowed from canals into alleys and homes, as if the ancient city was finally being consumed by the sea. Rats that hadn't yet found shelter ran across Max's path or were swept along in the rising water swilling into every crack and crevice.

In the splatters of lightning that punctuated the darkness, shadows moved in and out of doorways and around corners, like thieves stealing into the night. Max stopped running and took shelter beneath the stone archway of a church. Drips from the giant stone cross above fell like a fountain around her. She folded her arms across her chest and jiggled her feet in her wet shoes, desperate to drive away the aching cold gnawing into her bones.

Another lightning flash splintered into the alley, creating even more shadows, as if Max was surrounded by a gang of faceless strangers.

But one shadow was real. Its distorted human shape slithered along a darkened wall as if preparing to pounce.

Max knew the figure was here for her.

She took a deep breath and ran. The shadow followed.

She turned to catch a glimpse of him but he was hidden in the folds of the miserable night and a swirling black cloak, until lightning snagged at his face and Max saw him. He had sharpened cheekbones, a pencil-thin moustache, and a sneer chiselled out of pure malice.

The alley narrowed into a sharp turn. Max jumped over a small pot of limp, drowned flowers and rounded the corner, but halted, arms flailing, as she realized her fate.

The alley ended abruptly against the swirling waters of a canal.

Max's pursuer stopped and edged slowly closer. Thick, sticky rain fell down Max's face like waves of tears. The canal boiled before her like a blackened cauldron, but it was what was above it that stopped her heart.

Linden was suspended from a balcony, twirling at the end of a rope against the cruel whips of wind and rain.

'Save me, Max!' he yelled over the ear-crushing deluge.

It was a set-up. She thought she was outrunning her pursuer, when she was really being driven to a terrible end. Max fought against the storm and the stabbing fear of losing her friend for ever.

'I'm coming, Linden. Hold on.'

But then her cloaked pursuer took out a knife and with precise marksmanship threw it at Linden's rope, severing it in two. Linden fell into the canal and was swept towards the swollen waters of Venice's darkened harbour.

'No!'

A deep-throated laugh cut through the air as Max ran forward, balancing at the water's edge as she tried to see her friend. Where was he? Which wave was he caught under? She had to find him and pull him out before it was too late. Before—

Max leapt up, gasping for breath as water washed down her face and onto her clothes. Her mind was full of Venetian streets and canals, rain and blinding lightning strikes, but as she wiped her dripping hair from her eyes and focused on what was around her, she realized she was in the sleep-out at Mindawarra.

She also saw the reason for her own private downpour.

'You!' she snapped at one of Geraldine's chicks, which was innocently pecking its way along the windowsill above her bed. The same windowsill that up until moments before had been holding a glass of water.

Geraldine was a chicken who decided from the moment they met that Max was there for her to harass. Linden thought she was crazy to think a chicken could get personal, but Max knew it was true. She could see it in the bird's beady eyes. Geraldine had created chicken poo traps, spooked Max by flying at her in a flapping frenzy, and then had three chicks she was training to do the same.

Max didn't have a great affinity with the animal kingdom, but when it came to this particular feathered part, lines had been drawn for outright war. A kind of guerrilla war, only in this case it was a chicken war.

She reached for the towel Ben had left on the end of her bed and wiped her face and pyjamas. She'd arrived in Mindawarra the night before. Her mother's wedding was only weeks away and despite demanding Max's help, she'd now decided she was too busy with the final preparations and it would be best if Max went to the country. Only when Max's mum had said 'too busy', what she really meant was that Max was too clumsy.

So what if she'd spilt a little raspberry juice on her mother's favourite rug and accidentally left the iron on so Aidan burnt his hand; and the shower curtain was old anyway, so the candle burning it to a small pile of blackened soot was really only doing them all a favour.

Her mother, of course, hadn't seen it like that, and Max was sent away as quickly as it could be arranged. Normally Max loved every chance to be away from her mother and her manic ways, but she'd actually started to enjoy being with her, and even though she still wasn't ecstatic about the idea of Aidan being her stepdad, the wedding was starting to sound like fun.

That is, if she was still invited.

A high-pitched cheeping interrupted her thoughts.

'I bet you stand in front of the mirror practising looking innocent, don't you?' Max glared at the young chick prancing up and down the windowsill as if in some kind of victory parade. 'You lice-infested, ground-scratching . . .'

But just then a drop of water slid from her hair

onto her face, and the last part of the dream crept into her mind.

The part where Linden fell into the canal.

And she couldn't save him.

She'd been having dreams like this since she saw Linden fall to his death in Blue's torture chamber in Hollywood. He fell because Max couldn't control her temper and Blue decided to take it out on Linden.*

They were always the same kind of dreams: Max being chased until she came across Linden suspended from something. A cliff, a building, a scaffold. And then he'd fall.

When they went on their first mission, Linden had made them say a pact promising to look out for each other. It had seemed silly, even embarrassing, but after what happened to him, Max had made her own pact: that she'd be there for Linden always.

And that she'd curb her temper.

Max heard the sound of tearing paper and looked down. Geraldine was showing her young chick how to use her beak to tear the pages of Max's spy notebook.

* See *Max Remy Spy Force: The Hollywood Mission*

'That's it!' Max threw the towel aside and went to leap out of bed, but as she did her foot got tangled in the sheets and she landed headfirst on the floor in a sodden mess.

'There are easier ways to get up, you know.'

Max sighed into a soggy spot on her blanket. 'Why does there always seem to be someone around to watch me make a fool of myself?' she mumbled as she tried to sit upright.

'You mean these things don't happen when you're on your own?' Linden crunched into some peanut butter toast while Ralph wagged his tail beside him.

'Of course not,' Max lied, then frowned.

Ralph whined as if he sensed something was wrong.

'Are you OK?' Linden asked.

Max looked at the mess around her and wondered where to start.

'I had a nightmare.'

'What about?'

'All sorts of stuff.' Max still felt bad bringing up Linden's death with him.

'Mum used to say nightmares usually mean there's something going on in our lives we're unhappy about.'

Geraldine chose that moment to cackle loudly, her feet still firmly planted on Max's mauled spybook. Max reached over and grabbed the book, sending Geraldine squawking for cover.

'Hey,' Linden said, 'I think your palm computer has an incoming message.'

Max sighed. She always seemed to get the most important messages when she was in her pyjamas.

She turned on her computer and activated the link.

It was Steinberger, Spy Force's Administration Manager. 'Ah, Max and Linden. Great to see you again. Having a bit of a sleep-in, were you, Max?'

'Kind of.' Since the nightmares had started, she'd been sleeping badly and usually woke up late.

'Well, I think I have some news for you that you're going to find very exciting.'

'Excellent. What is it?' Linden gave the last of his toast to Ralph and took an apple from his pocket.

Before Steinberger could continue, Ben and Eleanor walked into the room, wondering why Linden was taking so long getting Max to breakfast.

'Steinby! How are you, you old sausage?'

'Very well thank you, Ben. Hello, Eleanor.'

'Morning, Steinberger.' Eleanor stood behind

Ralph and ruffled his fur. 'How's everyone at the Force?'

'Couldn't be better. Smooth sailing on all fronts, and last night was the Spy Industry Bowling Championship.'

'Let me guess,' Eleanor smiled knowingly. 'Quimby won?'

'Of course. Put those funny-looking shoes on her and she can do no wrong. Oh, but that reminds me. She's invented a new range of foldaway, inflatable vehicles, and we'd like Max and Linden to come to HQ to do a little training.'

'Training?' The colour drained from Max's face like water from an unplugged bath. The last time she'd done training, she might as well have worn a neon sign around her neck saying 'Mobile Danger Zone'.

'Yes, Max, but this time I think you're really going to enjoy it.' Steinberger loved Spy Force and his unstoppable sense of optimism would make the Force millions if they could package it and sell it.

'Sure,' Linden said in between chomps. 'When?'

'Today, if you're free.'

'Sounds good. Will they be back for dinner?'

Ben asked, as if kids all over the world got this request every day.

'Most certainly. A few hours should do it, I'd say.'

Linden's food radar spiked into life. 'What are we having?'

'Lasagne.' Ben smiled broadly.

Linden sagged at the possibility of missing out on his favourite dish. 'Really? Lasagne?'

'It'll be here when you get back,' Eleanor promised.

'Excellent,' Steinberger cried. 'We'll see you here in about an hour.'

Max showered and got into some dry, chicken-free clothes, and, despite her excitement, she managed to finish a little breakfast before the four of them made their way to the yard to prepare for their trip to Spy Force Headquarters in London.

Max saw Larry moving cardboard boxes around his pen. Larry was Ben and Eleanor's pig and according to them, the weather could be predicted by his behaviour.

'Don't tell me,' Max began. 'There's going to be a storm.'

'Nope,' Ben answered.

'A flood?'

'Not likely,' Eleanor replied.

'Rain? A heatwave? A tornado?'

'He acts in other ways for those,' Linden added.

'What is it then?'

'Ernie Sullivan's coming to visit today with his pig Gwenda and Larry wants to impress her.' Ben watched as Larry's cardboard construction came together. 'He's doing a pretty good job of it, too.'

'He's sweet on Gwenda,' Eleanor leant towards Max and whispered. 'Only he doesn't like us making a fuss about it.'

Max looked at the three people standing in front of her admiring their pig and decided that was all she wanted to hear about Larry's love life. 'Time to go, I guess.'

They walked a little further away from the house before stopping.

'This should be a good place.' Ben pulled the original Time and Space Machine from his pocket. He and Eleanor had given it to Max as a present, but took it back after Max misused the Matter Transporter Mark II on their last mission.*

'Travel carefully.' Ben had a way of getting

* See *Max Remy Spy Force: The Hollywood Mission*

emotional at goodbyes and his eyes were already quivering with tears.

'We will. I promise.' After disappointing them during their Hollywood mission, Max was determined not to let them down again.

Eleanor patted Ralph's head as he stood calmly at her side. There was a time when he'd almost kill Max just saying hello, but since Linden had trained him, he was much more restrained.

'See you, buddy. You've done well.' Linden nuzzled his nose into the fur on Ralph's head, knowing he would have loved a pre-flight rumble.

Max prepared the machine to transport them to Spy Force as Linden stood beside her.

'Be careful on those new vehicles,' Ben cautioned. Ralph edged forward and whined in agreement.

'OK,' Max answered.

'And come home as soon as it's all over.' Ben's voice rose higher as Ralph let out a small yelp.

'Gotta go now.' Max was keen to avoid any situation where she'd have to face an adult crying, but just as they were about to leave, Ralph couldn't contain himself any longer and leapt at her for a final goodbye. The two rolled onto the ground in an exploding whorl of dust.

'Get off me!' Max's voice gurgled from the confusion of legs, fur, and dirt.

Ben and Linden finally managed to drag Ralph off as Eleanor helped a dishevelled and dirt-streaked Max to her feet.

'Boy, he's really going to miss you.' A clean, unrumpled Linden smiled at Max.

Ralph whimpered quietly, agreeing with Linden but knowing he'd probably overdone it.

Max glared at them both before looking down at the sorry mess her clothes were in. She'd been rolled in dirt, leaves, burrs, and, she noticed with a sigh, a giant cow-pat. Her palm computer then vibrated with a message. 'Great!' she moaned. 'Steinberger is standing by for our arrival and I look like I've been run over by a truck!'

'You can borrow my jacket.' Ben held out his checked flannelette farm shirt, full of patched holes and stains from last night's dinner.

'Thanks, but I think we'll just go,' Max said, before spitting out a feather. She gave Ralph one last look and sighed. She knew he meant well, but she also knew that her promise to Linden to control her temper was shaping up to be the hardest promise she'd ever made. But she *had* promised, so this time when she took Linden's hand, she knew it was different, that watching him die had somehow changed her for ever.

'Ready?' she beamed, a stick of hay poking out of her hair.

'Ready,' Linden replied.

'Transport.'

As Ben sniffed and sadly blew his nose, a green flash of light ballooned around them, followed by a quiet 'fffttt' and a small haze of dust.

CHAPTER 2
THE NEW AGENT

The Vehicular All-Response Tower at Spy Force, or VART for short, was swarming with movement. Maintenance crews ferreted under choppers, crawled over submarines, and recharged small golf-buggy type vehicles, while agents returning from newly completed missions stepped out of various kinds of transporters and a group of people in suits were ferried around as if they were on some kind of tour.

Somewhere in the middle of all this there was a brief flash of fluorescent light and tiny sparks of colour fell to the ground like fireworks as Max and Linden gently descended.

Max had never seen the VART so busy, which made it no surprise that fate had chosen now for her to arrive in all her farm-smeared splendour.

'Wow! Look at this place.' Linden gaped at the frenzy around him while Max did her best to unmangle and de-dust her clothes.

'This place is packed!' Linden was oblivious to Max's frantic attempt at grooming. 'There are people everywhere. It's like landing in the middle of a royal show.'

Max moved behind Linden and swiped a handkerchief at the clump of cow poo that had plastered itself to her behind.

'It's like the whole of Spy Force has come out just to—'

'Witness the last few seconds of your life?' Max clipped.

Linden finally got it. 'No.'

Steinberger's long legs came striding along the metal boardwalk that led into the VART. He was holding out his stopwatch and wearing a proud grin as he came to a standstill before them.

'Well done. Thirteen and a half seconds. Even faster than before. Must have had the wind behind you, eh?' He laughed at his joke. 'It's so very good to see you both again. Today is going to be exciting.' He craned his head around Linden to get a better view of Max. 'That's a unique outfit, Max. It's so hard to keep up with what the youth are wearing these days.'

Linden tried to give him a look to stop him but he kept going.

'It suits you. Kind of crushed chic, is it?'

Linden's eyes were darting all over, warning him not to say any more, but Max gave him a big toothy smile and said, 'Thanks, Steinberger.'

She took another deep breath and offered Linden a look that said, 'See, I can do it.' Linden smiled back. He knew Max and her temper came as a boxed set and it wasn't going to be easy for her to let it go.

Steinberger rubbed his hands vigorously. 'Time to test those new vehicles, eh?'

He turned and led the way towards the exit, chatting endlessly to Linden. Max lagged behind with her new splatter look, but as she followed, she began to smile. Spy Force still made her feel as if she was somewhere special. It made her want to whisper, as if she was walking through a cathedral. As if she was . . .

'Oooph!'

Max's awe was ended by a well-pressed and over-cologned suit.

'Would it be too much trouble to look where you're going?' Max knew she'd run into him, but after a morning where she couldn't do anything right, she had to yell at someone.

The suited man stood among a group of silent people, who were all now staring at Max.

'I'm so sorry. Are you OK?' Mr Cologne answered in a super-concerned voice.

This burned Max even more. He had every right to be upset with her and instead he was standing in front of her being all sugar-coated.

'Fine,' she mumbled, realizing she could do

without the audience. She hurried after Linden and Steinberger.

'Who are they?' Linden asked Steinberger when Max had caught up with them.

'New recruits.' They looked back at the well-dressed group being shown through the VART. 'Specially taught for months in training centres all over the world before even being allowed to enter Spy Force Headquarters.'

'But we . . .' Linden began.

'I know. You and Max were inducted much sooner, but you had also tackled Blue and won. There aren't many spies who can say that.'

'You hear that?' Linden nudged Max. 'We're special.'

Max simmered in a rush of warmth. She loved being a spy and Linden was the perfect spy partner. Together they'd been dangled over huge vats of jelly, survived the evil workings of the Nightmare Vortex, and even managed to cheat death.

'These recruits have been handpicked by Harrison as the best of the current training programme and I have no doubt each one will be a top-notch agent,' Steinberger announced. 'Now, on to the testing area. The place where our brilliant

Quimby tests her new inventions. This is going to be fun!'

Before she left, Max took one last look at the VART and caught sight of the cologne guy standing apart from the others, staring at her, as if he was studying her every move. When he saw her looking, he immediately turned away and joined the others in questioning their instructor.

Why was he looking at her and what did he want? Maybe he was planning something evil? Harrison had warned her to be careful judging other people before she knew all the facts, but she couldn't ignore the strange feeling that crept over her when she saw him staring at her.

She shook it off and quickly turned away to join Steinberger and Linden, unaware that the new recruit had turned back and was watching her again.

CHAPTER 3

INFLATABLE VEHICLES AND AN URGENT CALL FROM HARRISON

'Just stare directly at the wall and stand as still as you can.'

'Steinberger, are you sure we have to do this?' Max sighed.

'Oh yes, most definitely.'

'But won't we end up in the Plantorium?'

'This part of the Wall will take us directly to Quimby.'

The Wall of Goodness. The only object in Spy Force Max had a personality clash with.

Max, Linden, and Steinberger stared at the solid stone wall, waiting for the atoms to start reconfiguring in its jelly-like identification process.

'Come and get me, Wall.' With Linden, of course, there was no clash. He and the Wall might as well have been old soccer buddies.

'You will notice the Wall start to move—' Steinberger began.

'We know, like jelly. Can you hurry it up?' If Max had to do this she wanted it to be fast.

After a few more seconds, the Wall wavered in front of them before reaching out and slowly enveloping them. Linden and Steinberger were sucked through in a quiet, no-fuss slurp, while Max's dirt-smeared body was jiggled, massaged, and wrestled like a rugby ball during a grand final.

Then it stopped.

'Hey, Wall, maybe you could choose some other time to flake out. I've got work to do.'

Nothing.

Max stood glued in her Wall-surrounded state. Maybe this time she really wouldn't get through. What was the Wall doing? Why wasn't it moving? How come . . .

'Aaaaah!'

The Wall finally chose to spit her out the other side and she was sent sprawling across the highly polished lab floor, stopping in front of a small, nondescript red door and several pairs of feet.

'Max! How lovely to see you again. Now we can get started.' Quimby stared down at her with her hands in her lab coat and a bright purple scarf on her head attempting to hold in her long unruly hair. Max dragged her ego-dinted body from the ground and followed the inventor as she unlocked the door and opened it onto the testing area.

'What do you think?' Steinberger asked in his chuffed kind of way.

Max stared. It wasn't quite the VART-like hangar full of gadgets and vehicles that she'd imagined.

'It's a lake.' She gazed at the vast and seemingly

endless blue expanse of water before her, fringed with grass and trees.

'It is. Kind of.' Quimby smiled as a fish splashed through the surface and somersaulted before falling back into the water.

'But we're in the middle of London!' Linden needed to make sure the Wall of Goodness hadn't spat them into a different place.

Quimby's face exploded in a smile of excitement. 'Yes, we are, but with a clever mix of physics and nature, we've created the naturescape you see before you. You see, what we did . . .'

Quimby explained her work to the others but Max heard none of it as she strode along the bank of the lake.

'Is there an end to this?' Max walked on, but before Quimby could say anything to stop her, her head rebounded off something hard.

'Ow!'

'Looks like there is,' Linden said.

Quimby tried to conceal a smile. 'It does look like it's never-ending, but that's because its borders are carefully concealed.'

'Isn't that amazing?' Steinberger gasped.

'Yeah. Amazing.' Max rubbed her head.

'The machines we test in this area have

built-in sensors so they automatically stop when they approach solid objects. Perfect for manoeuvring through darkened places or coming up against invisible objects.'

'Have you got any of those sensors for Max?' Linden asked with a grin that was trying to break into a laugh.

'It can be arranged.' Quimby wasn't so successful and let loose a small chuckling gasp.

'Hello, everyone.'

At the sound of that voice Max felt as if her whole body had been bungy-jumped. Her pulse quickened, her mind scrambled, and her mouth, as usual in these situations, stopped working.

'Hi, Alex,' chorused everyone except Max.

'Excellent to see you, Alex.' A piece of long dark hair fell into Quimby's eyes and she tried to tuck it into her scarf, with very little success. 'Ready for the demonstration?'

'Absolutely.' Alex Crane was the best agent in the Force and had the ability to look professional and casual at the same time. 'Hello, Max. Nice to see you again.'

Alex was intelligent, good-looking, and always in control. Max, on the other hand, had trouble just trying to stand up. 'I . . . ah . . . it's . . .' She and

Alex had last been together on a mission to save the Annual Spy Awards Night from a volcano Mr Blue had made active. They did it, but not before Max almost got them both killed.*

Everyone was looking at her, including Alex, waiting for her to say something. Say anything, she ordered her brain. 'Ah . . . um . . . nice shoes.'

Alex looked down at her Spy Force-issue trainers. 'Thanks.'

'Let me show you what we're really here to see.' Quimby turned to continue the demonstration but she was overcome by a yawn. 'Excuse me. I'm terribly sorry. There've been a few late nights trying to get the vehicles ready for your visit. Follow me.'

'It's Alex,' Max whispered to Linden.

'I noticed,' Linden replied easily.

'She said it was nice to see me.' Max's admiration for Alex had the ability to make her disappear into a cloud of very non-Max behaviour.

'Max,' Linden protested, 'I always think it's nice to see you.'

'Did you hear her say it?' Max was beaming.

'Yeah.' Linden gave up for now.

Quimby took a small red rubber cube from her

*See *Max Remy Spy Force: The Nightmare Vortex*

lab coat. 'This is going to revolutionize travel for Spy Force agents everywhere. We've been working on it for years and now it's finally ready. Agents, I give you the Felani.'

Linden stared. 'It's a little small, isn't it?'

'Watch.' Quimby held out the rubber cube as if it were a rare diamond. She gave her hand a shake and threw the cube into the air. It unfolded balloon-like into a sleek sports car beside them.

'Isn't she beautiful?'

Linden breathed a quiet sigh. 'I'm going to be so hard to impress for the rest of the day.'

'You might want to close your mouth before the wind changes,' Max cautioned him. 'I'm not having a spy partner who could double as a fly catcher.'

Linden closed his mouth and smiled. 'Good joke.'

'Thanks.' Max shrugged proudly.

Quimby continued. 'The Felani is part of a new range of Inflatable Foldaway Vehicles we've invented and is for your more stylish encounters. Capable of ultra-high speeds, its wheels contain countless brush-like projections, much like the toes of a gecko, that create friction, enabling super grip on all kinds of surfaces,' and here Quimby flashed a wicked grin, 'as well as the ability to navigate non-horizontal surfaces.'

Linden's mouth dropped open again. 'So . . . it can scale . . .' His mind filled with the possibilities, 'walls, buildings, bridges?'

'For starters.' Quimby's mischievous smile got even cheekier. 'But that's not all.'

The agents followed Quimby as she walked over to a line of other vehicles parked at the edge of the lake.

'The vehicles are tough, resilient, and able to withstand a wide range of temperatures, air pressures, and forces. They are also equipped with Irene's invisibility formula, but unlike the Invisible Jet, it is stored in a secret compartment in the engine of the vehicle. All you need to do is press this button here.' Quimby leant into one of the vehicles and pressed a small button on the dashboard, releasing a soft hissing sound. 'It sends a parachute-shaped spray of serum over the vehicle and makes it invisible within seconds. This is a great addition to our vehicles for when you need to make a quick, unseen exit.'

The vehicle disappeared completely, as if swallowed by an invisible wave.

'I have got to get one of those,' Linden sighed.

'What, for all those baddies about to invade Mindawarra?' Max teased.

'It may look like a sleepy town,' Linden's eyes darted from side to side, 'but who knows what danger lurks behind those cow sheds?'

Max raised a crooked eyebrow at Linden as Quimby went on.

'The Inflatable Foldaway Vehicles also come in other types: the Aqua Buggy for expert manoeuvring on land and water; the Mountain Climber for those hard-to-get-to places up or down the sides of cliffs; and the Heliocraft, perfect for making quick getaways by air and also for flying in or out of confined spaces. Your Personal Flying Device can already carry you small distances, but for more challenging leaps, you'll need one of these.' Quimby proudly turned to her small audience.

'Ah,' she said to someone behind them, 'just in time for the rest of the explanation.'

They all turned to see a sharply-dressed man with perfect hair and teeth so white Max almost needed sunglasses to cut out the glare.

It was the cologne guy! What was he doing here?

'Sorry I'm late. I had to help Sleek with the Invisible Jet.'

'This is Agent Suave,' Steinberger said, as if he was introducing his long-lost son. 'One of our newest agents to the Force. After months of highly rigorous training and some of the toughest of tests, I'm proud to say he came out as one of the best recruits we've ever admitted. Besides Alex, of course.'

Steinberger gave Alex a warm look as Suave pushed a perfect wave of hair from his forehead.

'And from what I saw while Alex was training me, that's the biggest compliment I could have hoped for.' Suave offered Alex a boyishly good-looking smile that could have melted glaciers.

'This guy has no idea,' whispered Max to Linden. 'Alex hates all that charm stuff.'

'I can't wait until we have the chance to work together,' Suave added, gazing into Alex's eyes as if he was in a trance.

'This guy really doesn't get it,' Max scoffed quietly.

But then Alex did something Max had never seen before. She blushed.

'Me too,' Alex replied quietly.

Steinberger continued. 'Suave is an expert in extreme response action and in the short time he's been training with Sleek to learn the ins and outs of the vehicles in the VART, he's displayed quite some skill.'

'Just trying to do my best.' Suave looked down modestly.

'And these two fine agents,' Steinberger said, 'are Max Remy and Linden Franklin.'

'Max and Linden!' Suave seemed to inflate with enthusiasm. 'You two are famous. I've heard such great things about you both.'

Max stared at the new agent. He was perfect. He dressed well, had great manners, and always seemed to say the right thing.

'Agent Smarm, was it?' she asked innocently.

'Agent Suave, actually,' he said, completely missing her insult. 'And Linden. It is such a pleasure to meet you. I hear you're a natural at everything you do. Let me shake your hand.' Linden offered his hand and the two shook as if they were best friends.

'Suave has been training in the Inflatables all week.' Quimby smiled proudly. 'And has a talent that is astounding.'

Of course he has, Max thought as she looked at his confident yet humble smile.

'So if you need any tips on operating the vehicles, Alex and Suave are the ones to ask. Max, would you like to try one out?' Quimby asked.

Max's head jerked towards Quimby.

That was the last thing she wanted. Max knew

it would just be another chance to show Alex and this new guy how clumsy she was, but she also didn't want to appear afraid. 'Sure.'

'Brilliant! Let's try this one.'

Quimby led Max to a blue-green beetle-type car with its thick front wheels parked on the edge of the lake. She pulled a miniature remote control from her coat, pressed a small button and watched as the doors opened upwards. They both stepped into the vehicle and buckled themselves in. The doors closed quietly over them.

'Nice, eh?' Quimby started the engine. The smooth dashboard of the car came to life in a red glowing collection of dials, readings, and buttons. She put it into first gear.

'Shouldn't we be in reverse?' Max pressed her back against her seat, uneasy about being so close to the water's edge.

Quimby smiled the way she did when she had something great to unveil, and before Max could say anything else, she drove off the boardwalk straight into the water.

'Aaah!' Max screamed and shut her eyes tight, waiting for the water to swirl around her as she envisioned her life ending at the bottom of a slimy fish-filled lake.

Quimby held on to the steering wheel, her smile as wide as the windscreen, which was filled with all sorts of fish and other non-roadworthy creatures.

'Max, you've got to see this,' she cried.

Realizing she was still dry and not gasping for breath, Max squinted open her eyes just in time to see a giant catfish swim by.

'What do you think of the Aqua Buggy?' Quimby enthused.

Max stared quietly, relieved she wasn't going to become a muddied fossil in the bottom of the lake.

'It's the first of its kind. I'm very proud of it.'

They navigated their way around rocks, passing schools of fish and swaying reeds. After the thump of Max's heart had calmed down, it was actually quite peaceful.

'It's really good,' she finally managed.

'It's watertight, temperature-controlled, and runs on a super-concentrate plant fuel that will last for up to ten days underwater. On land, its super-grip wheels and powerful engine enable it to handle all terrains. Sand, mud, gravel. Anything. Hold on.'

Quimby turned sharply and manoeuvred the

Aqua Buggy up a muddy bank and back to the others.

'How was it?' Linden asked. Max was about to answer when she saw Alex laughing at something smarm-boy had said.

'I think we did OK,' Quimby answered for the young agent.

'Excellent!' Steinberger said before he was interrupted by a light on his palm computer. 'Excuse me.' He stepped away to take the message.

Max kept her eyes on Alex and Suave as she opened her door, but as she stepped out she tripped on the side of the buggy and fell headlong onto the pier. Right at Suave's impossibly shiny shoes.

'Let me help you there, Max,' he offered.

He began to lean over but Max stood up before he could touch her. 'I'm fine, thanks,' she said, reeling from having made a fool of herself once again.

'Thanks for the demonstration, Quimby,' Alex said. 'I have been requested to show Suave the Library and talk him through previous Spy Force missions.'

'And I couldn't think of a finer guide.' Suave let rip another toothpaste smile.

And the worst thing was, Alex fell for it! She blushed. Again. This was too much.

'That's fine,' Quimby said. 'Max and Linden have quite a few more vehicles to test before they leave.'

'Good to see you again, Max and Linden,' Alex smiled.

OK, brain, thought Max, here's your chance. It's time to show Suave you can be just as cool, calm, and confident as he is.

'Ahhh . . . it was . . . yeah,' she said out loud.

Good one, brain. That showed them. Max cursed her brain for never working when she really needed it to.

Suave stepped aside in an after-you gesture that Alex accepted and the two walked off with conspiratorial whisperings as if they were long-time spy partners.

Quimby pushed a piece of hair under her scarf and pulled out her notebook to decide which vehicle to test next.

Max stared after Alex and Suave. 'Why can't Alex see he's a jerk?'

'He seems all right.' Linden took a cheese stick from his pocket. 'Want some?'

Max kept staring, not noticing Linden's offer. 'Just look at him. Anyone can tell he's a fake. The accent, the swagger, the overpowering cologne—'

'The fact that he's so good at everything?'

'Yeah, the fact that he's—' Max stopped. Sometimes it was a pain that Linden could read her thoughts so well.

'Nothing tells you that you're being a little harsh?' he suggested.

'Yes, but I'm choosing to ignore that for now.'

Linden laughed. There was a time when Max and a sense of humour were as close as the north and south poles, but she seemed to be getting the hang of it.

Steinberger came back towards them, his face downcast with fear.

'What is it, Steinberger?' Max asked.

'Alex. Suave.' The two agents were about to leave the testing area, but rushed back at Steinberger's nervous call.

'Is something wrong?' Alex asked.

'Harrison has summoned us.' His previous excitement had been replaced by an air of disbelief. 'He said it's urgent.'

'What's happened?' Suave straightened up.

Steinberger stared at his miniature computer as if he had no idea how to say it.

'Harrison will explain when we get there.'

There was an air of un-Steinberger-like

nervousness about him as Linden, Max, Suave, and Alex followed the gangly legs of the Administration Manager out of the testing area towards the office of the Chief of Spy Force.

CHAPTER 4

THE SCENE OF THE CRIME

Harrison's office was buried deep within the subterranean levels of the agency. It was a top secret area accessible by a system of terracotta pots that doubled as elevators. Usually. But this time Steinberger bundled the agents into a tiny cupboard filled with musty clothes.

It was a tight fit and, to make it worse, Max was squeezed between Suave and his cologne and a bunch of mothballed coats, scarves, and trousers, all of which were starting to cut off the circulation to her brain.

'Where are we?' Max gasped through the strangulating smells.

Steinberger entered a code into a silver panel above the door handle.

'Harrison's wardrobe. It's the express route to his office that only a few people know about.'

Max sneezed as the mothballs ate into her nostrils like stink beetles.

Steinberger finished entering the code and the wardrobe jolted to life. The agents were flung downwards at full speed. After a few cramped plummeting moments, the wardrobe came to an abrupt standstill, sending the five agents tumbling into the gloomy atmosphere of the chief's office.

It was the same darkened room Max and

Linden remembered from their first visit to Spy Force. Tall ceilings, long stained-glass windows leading to nowhere, and deep leather sofas crowded with cushions. The walls were covered with paintings, certificates, and awards, the odd tennis racket and fishing rod, and imposing shelves of books. Max smiled as she spotted the garden gnomes and multi-sized terracotta pots.

And then there was Harrison, sitting behind his heavy oak desk. He seemed weighed down by a sad and disoriented look.

'Sir?' Steinberger asked with trepidation as he edged towards the desk.

Harrison didn't move. Max and Linden looked at each other as their bodies tingled with dread. Something was very wrong.

'Sir?' Alex tried this time.

'Yes? What? Ah, Alex, dear . . . you're here.' Harrison tried to feign an air of interest but it quickly became hidden under a blanket of gloom.

'What's happened, sir?' Alex had never seen her boss like this.

'Come with me.'

With heavy footsteps he led them out into the red-carpeted foyer. Max tried to push down a deep black fear.

Harrison stopped before a tall glass cabinet, filled with a blue silken cloth nestling in a dim glow. In the centre of the cloth was a hollow imprint.

'It's gone.' Harrison flinched as if even the reminder of the crime was painful to him. 'The original Spy Force manual has been stolen.'

Linden remembered the first time they'd seen the cabinet and what Steinberger had told them about it. 'It contains the very essence of the Force itself,' he repeated from memory.

Steinberger offered Linden a small smile that quickly faded as the seriousness of what had happened fell even more heavily upon them.

'Only a few people know this, but if that book falls into the wrong hands, it could be disastrous.' Harrison suddenly stiffened. 'It must be found.'

'Can't you have another one made up?' Max was hoping to ease the chief's distress, but he just looked lost, like someone who'd been drained of all their energy.

'What? Sorry . . . another one made up? That's impossible, Max. The original Spy Force manual had secret experiments fixed into the very fibres of its pages that are capable of transforming human existence as we blow it.' Harrison sighed. 'I mean, as we *know* it. It is written in an invisible ink developed by Frond and can only be read using a special lamp with a pink light fixed at a certain temperature level.'

'Maybe the person who stole it is unaware of this?' Suave offered.

'Thank you for your optimism, Suave, but whoever took the book knew the value of what they were doing.'

Harrison pointed to a piece of paper lying on the floor next to the cabinet. It read:

Thank you for your hidden secrets.
We promise to take good care of them.

'We must find it.' Although Harrison was trying to maintain a calm demeanour, a nervous edge had crept into his voice.

'What do we know about how it happened?' Alex's voice remained firm.

'Nothing yet. This glass cabinet is fingerprint sensitive, like your packs, and will only open to those with approved and programmed prints.'

'Whose prints, sir?' Linden asked warily.

Harrison looked uncomfortable.

'Myself, Steinberger . . .' Here he baulked. 'And Dretch.'

Max gave Linden a knowing look. She'd never liked Dretch, and he'd made it clear he didn't want them to be part of Spy Force. On one mission, Max had even suspected he'd sabotaged her equipment, hoping to bring about her premature end.*

Besides, with only three possible suspects, she could never believe it was Steinberger or Harrison who were to blame.

'I've ordered CRISP and the heads of each department to enforce a total lock-down. All agents have been told not to leave the Force tonight and to remain on full alert. Max, Linden, can you stay and help us out?'

Max straightened her spine and swept her shoulders back.

'We're ready to help out in any way we can.'

'Linden?'

'Absolutely.' Linden looked down at his watch and whispered to Max. 'You think it'll all be over in time for Ben's lasagne?' Max's scowl instantly made him reconsider. 'Not that it matters, of course.'

Four agents with the word CRISP stamped in white across their dark blue overalls jumped out of the terracotta pot elevator and ran into the foyer.

*See *Max Remy Spy Force: Spy Force Revealed*

They were from the Central Response Investigative Safety Patrol and were responsible for the internal security of Spy Force. They held stun guns firmly before them and scanned every corner of the foyer. When they were satisfied all was secure, they each took a place guarding each possible entry point. One of them turned to the elevator pot and gave a brief hand signal.

Another two agents then leapt out of the pot. They were wearing white jumpsuits and full headgear and were carrying box-shaped silver briefcases. After offering Harrison a brief nod, they got to work examining the cabinet. They put on huge magnifying eyewear, waved around small Geiger counters, and held out fingerprint analysers.

Harrison looked anxious, as if he was watching his favourite pet being operated on.

'Steinberger,' he said carefully. 'Organize the rosters for tonight and tomorrow. Ensure each department is taking all the necessary precautions and . . .'

It was as if he'd run out of knowing what to do. Steinberger stepped in.

'And get Irene on the case ready to feed everyone.'

'Yes . . . Irene.' Harrison's eyes rested on the two identification experts and his beloved glass cabinet. He stooped with weariness, and for the first time, Max thought he looked old.

CHAPTER 5
AGENT DRETCH AND SOME BAD NEWS FROM STEINBERGER

A fiercely chilled wind tore through the Old Town Square in the noble city of Prague, sending a whorl of sharpened ice and snow into a frenzied squall. The town shivered under its twisting, turning bursts as it forced its way into ancient castle turrets, beneath splintered roof beams, and along icy walls of huddled apartment blocks.

Weeks of unrelenting snow had cemented into thick white mounds beneath frosted windowsills, in narrow alleys, and on statues of important men. Above it all, the double spires of Tyn Church loomed like ornate, blackened spearheads. The church's stone walls and spires had withstood the winds of many winters, but this was one of the cruellest.

Max Remy fought against the wind that stormed into her, soaking a painful cold into her bones, but when she stopped and saw the spires, a grasping fear wrenched at her heart.

'Linden.' Her friend hung suspended between the spires.

Removing her thermal mitts, Max put on her super-grip gloves and began climbing the imposing building. She repeated their pact over and over, to drive away her fear of heights and the very real possibility of Linden being tossed into the last moments of his life. The climb was slow and laboured, each move sending a stabbing pain into her frozen hands.

When she reached one of the spires, she gripped its steel and only just managed to hold on against a vicious wind gust.

'Linden!'

His face was edged with a frozen blue and his eyes were dazed as his body fought to keep from passing out. The rope had been badly frayed and there was no way of knowing how long it would last.

She reached the top of the spire and held one arm out to him. With her super-grip gloves and her Abseiler, she'd be able to get them both to safety. But before she could move any further, the rope snapped. For a tiny moment their eyes locked.

'Linden!'

Her voice was swallowed by the wind, the same wind that buffeted Linden's body as he fell. Tumbling and falling . . . plunging headlong to—

The terracotta elevator came to an abrupt stop, flinging Max to the floor and the other agents on top of her.

'Have a nice . . . thank you for . . . please come again,' the melodious elevator voice stammered.

'Sorry about the ride.' Steinberger pulled himself up. 'The terracotta elevators have been playing up. The maintenance team have been called to repair them.'

'They'd better make it quick before someone gets killed.' Linden lifted himself from the floor and noticed Max's drained and frightened face.

'Max?'

He leant down to help her up.

'Yes?' She saw his outstretched hand and for a second she thought they were back at the double spires of Tyn Church.

'You need a hand?'

'Oh. Yeah. Thanks.'

With the news of the theft of the Spy Force manual, Max's head had filled with a daytime vision of her eerie nightmares. She wondered if she'd ever shake the terrible images and the sick feeling she got when she remembered she'd almost caused the death of her best friend.

'Are you sure you're OK?'

'Yeah.' Max took Linden's hand and stood up. 'Wasn't expecting the rough landing.'

Linden smiled, but he could tell there was something else worrying her.

They slipped through the partially opened doors of the elevator into a flurry of agents moving in all directions and standing in dark corners talking to each other in whispers. The air was goosebumped with unease.

Steinberger led them to the canteen, where Max and Linden would stay with Irene while he, Alex, and Suave went to check on the lock-down.

'We'll come with you,' Max offered.

'That's kind, Max, but when we've worked out our next move, we'll come and get you both. For now I'll leave you in Irene's hands. She knows you're coming and has prepared something special for you.'

Steinberger tried to smile, but the corners of his lips refused to curl upwards. He turned and left with Suave and Alex, saying no more. Max and Linden sat down at the nearest table.

'If I even think about food, I guarantee my stomach is not going to stay where it is.' Max breathed deeply, hoping to get rid of her queasiness.

'When I'm nervous the best thing to calm me down is food.' Linden shrugged a little guiltily.

Max gave him a half-smile. 'Yeah, I can see that.' Suddenly she felt as if she'd been covered in a blanket of ice. 'Is it me or is it cold in here all of a sudden?' She rubbed her arms and looked at Linden, who didn't answer. 'Don't you feel cold?'

'A little.'

She heard the words, but Linden's mouth hadn't moved. Max was hoping the voice hadn't come from who she thought it belonged to. But it had.

Dretch!

The only agent in Spy Force who could cause Max to experience her own personal arctic winter. He stood beside her with his spaghetti hair drooping over his eyes, his bent body covered by its crumpled maroon coat.

Max opened her mouth but nothing happened. There was a deathly pause as Dretch stroked his cat, Delilah, with his long chicken-bone fingers. Delilah soaked up the attention while offering Max a steadfast glare.

'What are you doing here?' Dretch growled.

'We . . . er . . . Steinberger said I . . . ah . . .'

Max stumbled over her words just as Irene walked into the canteen and offered one of her best duvet-warm smiles. 'There you are, you two. Steinby said you were coming. And Dretch, lovely to see you as always. Freezer fixed?'

Dretch offered a small groan and a nod.

'Knew you'd do it.' Irene clapped her hands.

'Now all three of you will have the honour of sampling a few new recipes from the kitchen. I'll just go and get them.'

Irene walked to the kitchen, leaving an awkward Dretch standing by Max. She could tell he wanted to leave, but the temptation of Irene's food held him back.

'I've got a bad feeling about this business.' Dretch pulled out a chair and grudgingly sat next to them. Max shivered even more, as if a glacier had been shipped in and parked beside her. 'There's something about this business that has *inside* job written all over it.'

Of course it was an inside job, Max thought, and with what we know about the fingerprints, I bet I'm staring at the guy on the inside right now.

'Do you think so, Dretch?' Linden asked.

'It's too clean a job. Too thorough,' he rasped. His head spun around so Max faced the jagged scar that ran from his chin down his neck. 'What do you think?'

She flinched. 'I think . . . it seems . . . it was probably . . .' She had hoped if her mouth started saying something her brain would come up with the rest. It didn't.

Linden had a theory. 'I think you might be right. With CRISP's impenetrable security, the theft must have happened with the help of an insider, or at least inside information.'

'The trouble is, if you're right, we may be in much more trouble than we think,' predicted Max gloomily.

Max sat uneasily beside the rumpled agent. In the past, Dretch had made it clear he wanted nothing to do with them, so having him this close to her made her skin itch with tension.

'What do you think happened to the book?' she tried to ask with confidence.

Dretch lowered his voice until it resembled low rolling thunder before a storm. 'CRISP are masters at security, as Linden said, and with the Vibratron and the Wall of Goodness, as well as the multiple security cameras and Spy Force agents, it was either someone very clever,' his voice deepened to a snarl, 'or someone who knew exactly what they were doing.'

Irene pushed through the kitchen door and placed a tray of food on the table. 'That's one busy kitchen. It'll be just like the Spy Awards Night all over again.'*

*See *Max Remy Spy Force: The Nightmare Vortex*

Max noticed Irene's shoulders drop a little. 'Are you OK?'

'Yes, of course.' She perked up. 'There's a lot to do and with all that's happened I just don't feel my usual self. It's terrible news about the book.' Linden saw her smile slip briefly and he exchanged a concerned look with Max.

'Why don't I tell you about these new treats I've made?' Irene, like Linden, believed food helped in any crisis, and they both lightened at the mention of it.

Max stared at Dretch, looking for any giveaway signs that he was guilty.

'I've recently been trying out a new ingredient which I believe will take eating to a whole new level.' Irene was always in search of new flavours to add to her unusual gourmet creations and Frond from the Plantorium often helped her out from her supply of fresh organic herbs and spices.

'Go on, try one,' Irene invited them.

Linden surveyed the trays of food. There were green and purple muffins with silver icing, blue twisting pastries sprinkled with red powder, and some chocolate-covered shapes that resembled ants. He knew they'd taste good—Irene was a whizz when it came to food—but just as he was about to tuck in, Steinberger walked through the canteen door with a face full of bad news. He was followed by four CRISP agents.

'Steinby?' Irene was no longer able to hide her concern. 'What's wrong?'

Max and Linden could see Steinberger had the words on the edge of his tongue but there was something stopping him from saying them. Linden's skin prickled as the air filled with a light mist of unease.

'I . . . I . . .' Steinberger began.

Max was really nervous now. Only Frond, who Steinberger had a crush on, could make him this bumbling and she was nowhere to be seen.

'I'm afraid I have some bad news.' Steinberger looked at the ground before turning to Dretch. 'Agent Maximus Dretch, by the authority vested in me by the Chief of Spy Force, I am arresting you for the theft of the Spy Force manual.'

I knew it! Max thought. He is guilty!

Irene let out a small snort of incredulity. 'What are you talking about, Steinby? This is Dretch. Our friend. He's been with the Force for over twenty years and has been its most loyal agent . . .'

She stopped as the CRISP team moved in and handcuffed the maroon-coated agent. Dretch offered no resistance. With only three sets of prints capable of opening the cabinet, he knew he would be singled out.

The handcuffs were clicked into place and Dretch was firmly positioned in the grip of the CRISP team, who awaited their next command. He locked eyes with Steinberger.

'I didn't do it,' Dretch muttered.

I'll bet you didn't, Max sniffed silently.

Steinberger let out a small sigh and whispered, 'I'm sorry, Maximus.'

Dretch slowly dropped his head. He looked forlorn and small beside the burly CRISP agents.

Irene's eyes filled with tears. 'I'll bring you something to eat, Maximus.'

Dretch offered no indication he'd even heard her.

'Take him to the cells.' The order was given quietly and Dretch was marched away. Steinberger watched as one of his best friends was pinioned like a common traitor.

CHAPTER 6
GUILTY FINGERPRINTS AND A LETHAL SLEEP

Spy Force agents began streaming through the canteen doors for dinner. There was a heaviness in the air as if everyone was moving through water. Quiet footsteps made their way to the food counter and low-level whispering circled around them like fireflies.

Steinberger stared at the palm computer clutched in his hand as if he was waiting for an answer, an explanation to what seemed an impossibility. After Dretch had been handcuffed and taken away he'd stayed completely still.

'Steinby?' Irene asked quietly.

He didn't move.

'Steinby?' She gently placed a hand on his arm.

'Mmm?' He looked up.

'What happened?'

Steinberger drew a deep breath. 'Dretch's fingerprints were found all over the cabinet.' Max could tell he was having trouble believing what he'd just said. For her part, though, she'd always known Dretch was bad.

'Maybe he'd been there recently just to look at the book,' Irene offered, certain that Dretch was not involved. She turned to see that the line-up for food had grown longer. She stood to go and help. 'Steinby, you and I know he didn't do it. It'll all get sorted out sooner than you know. Now I'm going back to work.' She paused before adding, 'At least food still makes sense.'

'Do you really think Dretch did it?' Linden asked as agents swarmed around them in silent, hungry groups.

Steinberger let out a long sigh. 'No.' He let his forehead fall into his hands. 'But with the discovery of his fingerprints there was nothing else Harrison could do except order his arrest.'

'What about the security cameras?'

Steinberger's palm computer lit up with a message. He looked wary. 'That'll be the footage from the cameras now. I asked CRISP to mail it to me as soon as they had it.'

Steinberger pressed a few buttons to open the attachment. The vision revealed the foyer outside Harrison's office, with the untouched cabinet sitting solidly in the middle. The view flicked to different angles, all with the book as its central concern. Then they saw Dretch. He walked straight to the cabinet and pressed his hands against the glass for fingerprint identification. After a small green light was seen at the base of the cabinet he lifted the heavy glass, took out the book, and tucked it under his arm, then replaced the glass as if it was something he did every day.

Max and Linden stared at each other.

'So he did do it,' Max declared.

'But he said he didn't.' Linden thought Dretch had sounded sincere, but now that he'd seen the footage, it seemed Dretch was guilty.

'You'd think he'd at least be clever enough to dismantle the cameras,' Max scoffed.

Steinberger turned off his computer, his saddened eyes still fixed on the screen.

'I'm sorry, Steinberger.' Linden wanted to make him feel better. 'Just let Max and me know what you'd like us to do.'

Steinberger offered him a weak smile. 'Thanks, Linden.' He stood slowly. 'I'd better get back to it.'

A metallic clang and crash of crockery was heard from the kitchen. Steinberger, Max, and Linden ran to see what had happened. On opening the door, they saw Irene kneeling next to an agent who was lying on the floor, a mess of plates and pots surrounding her.

'What happened?' Max asked.

'It's Agent Steeple, my assistant. She just fell down. I noticed she was looking off-colour earlier, but when I asked if she was OK she said it was just the worry about the book. That's the thing about Spy Force personnel, they never give up.' Irene looked protectively at her assistant. 'I've called Finch,' she added as she placed the agent in the recovery position.

Finch was the Spy Force doctor, and he responded immediately to Irene's call. Within minutes he and two assistants barged through the kitchen doors, their hands gloved in latex and their white coats flying behind them. Finch swooped to the floor to examine the fallen agent.

Max, Linden, Irene, and Steinberger waited nervously for his diagnosis. Finch worked quietly, checking the patient over, his serious face not giving anything away.

Steinberger frowned. After what had happened today, a sharp feeling in his stomach told him this latest incident was not unrelated to the stolen Spy Force manual.

Finch paused in his examination and looked into the expectant faces of the agents surrounding him.

'What is it, Finch?' Steinberger knew by his expression that the prognosis wasn't good.

'I've seen this only once before while I was working in the jungles of Africa. Of course I will need to do tests, but from what I have gleaned from my initial examination, I'd say it could only be one thing.'

He looked down at the agent with a forlorn look but before Steinberger could ask what that one thing was, another commotion was heard from outside. Max ran to the door. 'Another agent has collapsed!'

Finch ran outside and examined the second fallen agent, then turned to his assistants. 'Take these agents to the infirmary and place them under quarantine.' The assistants immediately unfolded portable stretcher beds on wheeled stands and carefully lifted the agents on to them.

'Well, what is it?' The doctor's silence was twisting Steinberger's stomach into impossible knots.

'Come with me,' Finch called as he followed his assistants out of the canteen. 'I can tell you when I know more.'

A stillness fell over the canteen as the agents were left in an ominous silence. Max, Linden, and Steinberger hurriedly followed in the stretchers' wake. Max clenched and unclenched her hands, hoping the sick feeling in her stomach would be driven away by Finch's diagnosis, but somehow she knew things were about to become very serious.

CHAPTER 7
A DIRE PROGNOSIS

The observation room was separated from the rest of Finch's infirmary by a large, reinforced window. It gave a perfect view of the agent lying on the table. She was young and fit but unmoving, and with a grey pallor sweeping across her lifeless face, it seemed she'd been frozen in time. Since Finch had started his examination, several more agents on stretchers had been rushed into the infirmary.

Finch slowly lifted his stethoscope from the patient's chest and exhaled through his surgical mask. He looked up through the observation window towards the troubled faces of Max, Linden, Harrison, and Steinberger. He gave instructions to his medical staff before leaving the table and climbing the stairs to join them.

He lowered his mask, a growing disquiet marking his every move. 'Her heart is very weak,' he announced with a grim face. 'I'd only completed her regular check-up last week. She rated brilliantly in every category.'

He looked away sadly as if he was somehow to blame.

'What is it, Finch?' Harrison had left his office the moment he heard the news. He was prepared for the worst.

'It's either Trypanosomiasis or Chagas' Disease,' Finch answered.

A heavy pause fell between them.

'What's that?' Max asked.

'Sleeping sickness,' Harrison translated.

'Sleeping sickness is a real disease?' she asked with raised eyebrows.

'Most definitely. And not only is it real, but if left untreated, it can also be fatal.' Finch took a deep breath. 'Normally the disease is caused by a blood parasite that is transmitted by bites from the tsetse fly in Africa or the triatoma bug from South America.' He looked to Steinberger. 'Have any of the infected agents been near either continent in the last few months?'

Steinberger looked up the list of agent files in his palm computer. 'In the last year, the areas covered were the Swiss Alps, the caves of Cappadocia, the Black Forest in Germany, and the glaciers of New Zealand.'

'Nowhere near Africa or South America,' Finch spelt out, almost to himself. 'This could be more difficult than I thought.'

Harrison turned to Steinberger. 'Try and find a link between all the agents who have been struck down so far. Run a search on everywhere they've been and ask questions of their families that may give us some clue as to how they may have become ill.' He softened his voice. 'And Steinberger . . . be careful not to alarm them.'

Harrison felt a loyalty towards each Spy Force member as if they were family, and when any one of them was in peril his heart ached as if a small knife had cut into it.

'It's also possible that whatever caused the disease has made its way inside the Force,' he speculated. 'Contact maintenance and have them check all the air-conditioning units, and have Dretch check all vehicles and equipment for any foreign matter.'

There was an awkward pause as Steinberger looked up from his note-taking.

'I mean, coordinate Dretch's team to do it.' Harrison wasn't yet used to his friend being detained. He turned to Finch. 'How many are there now?'

'We have seven agents under our care at present. Three field agents and two more from the kitchen staff.'

Harrison looked through the glass at Agent Steeple on the observation table. 'Will they all be OK?'

'They're stable for now. I've given them an injection of one of Frond's Plantorium products which will stop the symptoms of the disease from getting worse. I've also put them on respirators as the illness is very taxing on the lungs, but it won't last for ever,' he warned. 'We have to discover the exact cause in order to provide a real cure. Otherwise . . .'

His unfinished sentence hung in the air with a deathly quiver until Harrison turned away from the glass and laid out his plan of action.

'Finch, contact Frond and tell her all you know. If there's anyone who can work out an antidote it will be her. Steinberger, you and I will need to start formulating a mission to locate and retrieve the Spy Force manual and get a brief to Quimby as soon as we can.' He then turned to Max and Linden. 'With the spectre of sleeping sickness in our midst, I'm afraid you won't be able to return home yet.'

Max stood taller. She wouldn't have left even if they'd tied her to a seat in the Invisible Jet and tried to fly her away.

'I'll contact Ben and Eleanor and ask them to cover for you while you're here.'

'What would you like us to do, sir?' Max almost saluted.

Harrison smiled. 'I know it may not sound very exciting, but with all the kitchen staff who have fallen ill, Irene will need your help.'

Max's heart lurched. She would have preferred to have gone with Harrison, to be in the front line for whatever was destabilizing the Force.

Two more patients were wheeled into the surgery. The medical team swept into action as Finch offered a small nod, refitted his mask, and went to their assistance.

Harrison approached the glass again and looked down on the infirmary. Max started to say goodbye but the look of quiet despair on his face stole her words from her. Linden gently touched her on the arm and they left in silence.

CHAPTER 8

A VILE PLAN AND A DEADLY GIFT

The waterlogged mop came down in a splashing frenzy just as Max entered the canteen doors with Linden.

'That's not good.' Linden winced as the grey soapy water soaked into Max's shoes.

Irene held the dripping culprit guiltily. Her face was red, her apron damp, and her chest heaving with her cleaning effort. She looked tired and rumpled, with her usual Irene shine hidden behind a nervous frown. 'I'm so sorry, Max.' There was the smallest crack in her voice that made Max want to reach out and wrap her in a hug.

'It's OK, Irene. We've come to help.'

Irene breathed deeply. 'And I'll be glad to have your company,' she replied with a flash of her old self as she picked up her bucket and led the way into the kitchen. 'Max, yours is the tea towel, and Linden, you get to put away.' Irene turned to a sink loaded with dishes and began a jovial whistle, but Max and Linden could tell her cheerfulness was just a cover.

'What do you think is responsible for all this sleeping sickness, Irene?' Linden asked.

'I've been thinking about that so much I think I've almost worn out a part of my brain.' Irene's attempt at a joke drew a sad smile on to her lips.

'Those agents are like my own kids. If anything was to happen to any one of them . . .' She turned back to the sink and began scrubbing a giant pot even harder.

'Finch reckons it's something they've come into contact with in the last few weeks. Flies or bugs that are normally found in Africa or South America.' Max picked up a large saucepan and began drying it with her tea towel.

Linden continued for her. 'All the agents it has struck have come from different units, have been on different assignments and none of them have been anywhere near those two continents.'

Irene turned to them with her eyebrows flipped high.

'Then it might be something inside Spy Force?'

'Harrison thinks it might be,' Max explained. 'He's having the place fully checked out.'

Linden picked up a casserole dish and made for a large shelf. 'So far they haven't found any common factor.'

Irene breathed a deep, resonating sigh.

'Well, at least among all this commotion there's one thing we can be sure of.' She took off her gloves and moved towards the ovens. 'I'm going to make sure everyone has lots of good food to eat.'

Something struck Max about what Linden and Irene had just said, as if her brain was trying to tell her something but she wasn't sure what. She watched as Irene took a tray of rich plum tarts from a cooling rack and assembled them on a plate.

'See what you think of these,' Irene said proudly. 'I've added a little something special to it that I'll bet my best pair of shoes will knock your socks off.'

Linden fell into his usual food-zombie mode at the sight of food. His mouth fell open and his tongue ran along his bottom lip wondering which one he should try first. He reached slowly forward and picked up a tart, still warm, full of thick overflowing plummy syrup.

But then something else happened in Max's brain. Something that told her Linden shouldn't eat the tart.

She leapt forward and swiped it out of Linden's hands, sending it skidding across the shiny floor like a jellied discus, leaving a red trail and a lilting disappointment in Linden's eyes.

'I know I should be thinking of things other than my stomach, Max, but honestly, my brain works better after I've eaten.'

Max *was* worried about Linden's stomach, but not in the way he thought.

'Not happy with the menu, Max?' Steinberger had just avoided the flying tart as he walked through the kitchen doors. 'Usually people can't get enough of Irene's food.'

Max's brain jolted again. 'I know,' she answered, before turning to Irene. 'Have there been any changes in the kitchen in the last few weeks?'

'Changes? Why do you ask?' Irene folded her arms across her chest, miffed that Max had thrown one of her prized creations across the floor.

'It's just an idea I have. Have there been any new staff? New cleaning products? New ingredients?'

Irene didn't like where Max's questions were headed.

'No, only the usual high quality, organic . . .' Irene stopped and her face paled to the colour of flour. She slowly spoke her next thoughts. 'Except for the new spice from Venezuela.'

'A new spice?' Steinberger felt a tremor of warning. 'Where did you get it?'

'It came with the last delivery of supplies from Susoka and Sons.'

Susoka and Sons was a food supplier that had

been checked out by Spy Force and given the all clear to be their official supplier.

'They'd sent it as a new sample to try out.'

'Did you have it tested?' Steinberger asked.

Irene paused. 'I usually give everything new I receive to Frond for testing, but I got so busy . . . and it was from Susoka so I thought . . . I never . . .' She bit her lip, unable to finish.

'What have you used it in?' Steinberger continued.

Irene was lost in trying to remember. 'The prawn soup, the mango muffins, the strawberry flambé . . .' She broke off.

'Do you know if the sick agents ate any of those dishes?' Linden asked gently, hating to see Irene so sad.

'I . . . I . . .' she began.

'Here's a list of agents.' Steinberger called up the files and photos of the sick agents on his palm computer and showed it to her.

Irene's floury complexion became even whiter. 'Yes.' She paused. 'All of them.'

'Are you sure?' Linden asked.

'I have a photographic memory for that kind of thing. I like to know the dishes each agent is partial to.'

'When did the ingredient arrive?' Max asked.

'About a week ago,' Irene whispered.

Max turned to Steinberger. 'When did Suave arrive?'

Steinberger's mouth went dry. 'Now, Max, I think it might be best not to jump to conclusions. It does happen that Agent Suave arrived a week ago, but with all the training and the security checks, he couldn't possibly have anything to do with . . .' His words fell away. With all that had happened in the last few hours, anything was suddenly very possible.

They stood in a silence laced with confusion. Spy Force was impenetrable. In all the years since it had been established, no one had ever managed to infiltrate it. Blue had come close but was stopped due to the efforts of the Wall of Goodness, which detected his evil intentions and caused him to be ejected from the Force.

'I'm sorry . . . I . . .' Irene's lower lip trembled. 'What have I done?'

'You haven't done anything,' Max said firmly. 'But someone else certainly has.'

'Is there any of the sample left?' Steinberger gently touched Irene's hand.

Her eyes only became sadder. 'I used it all up.'

'Do you still have the packet it came in?' Linden asked.

'Yes. It was a plain canvas bag. I kept it so I could reorder it.'

'Excellent,' Steinberger said. 'Hopefully there will be enough residue to complete a test. We don't have any time to lose. We must get it down to . . . to . . .' His eyes smouldered like two paraffin lamps and a quiet gasp passed his trembling lips. 'Frond . . . for analysis.'

Steinberger's hopeless crush on Frond, the head of the Plantorium, again sent his brain into a wordless wilderness.

'I'll get it straight away.'

Irene's voice jolted Steinberger back to reality. 'Yes. Yes.' He tapped on his palm computer. 'I'll get someone onto Susoka and Sons. Maybe they can give us some clues as to where this mysterious sample came from.'

Max and Linden watched as his fingers sped across the keys of his palm computer.

'Steinberger?' Max asked the question that was in both their minds. 'Spy Force is going to be OK, isn't it?'

The Administration Manager stopped typing and turned to the two young agents. 'Of course it is.

Spy Force has thwarted many threats and dangers in the past and so we will this one.'

Even though his words were delivered with a calm confidence, Max couldn't help noticing Steinberger's eyes, which were marked by a deep glow of apprehension.

CHAPTER 9
A MAN-EATING BLADDERWORT AND ANOTHER COLLAPSE

'Oh, great.'

For the second time that day Max found herself standing in front of the Wall of Goodness. She looked across at Irene, who was holding the canvas bag that had held the new sample, and knew it was the only way to the Plantorium from the kitchen.

Here goes another wasted clump of my life, she thought, as she stood in front of the Wall and waited for it to be difficult.

The goo process began and Max, Linden, Steinberger, and Irene became quickly enveloped by a sensation not unlike being dipped in lumpy custard.

And soon after, as Max expected, the Wall started being difficult.

'Oh no,' Irene gasped. 'I've made the Wall have doubts about letting us through, haven't I?'

'No.' Linden jiggled. 'It's Max. She and the Wall have this special relationship they've developed over time.'

Max tried to frown at Linden but the wall gurgled around the edges of her face, mushing it into all sorts of squished shapes.

Then, in a mass exit, all four of them were enveloped into the Wall's structure and spat out the other side into the Plantorium. They all quickly found their balance, but Linden noticed something strange about Max.

'Is it just me or do you seem shorter all of a sudden?'

Max looked down and saw she'd landed in a shallow swamp, completely soaking her recently mopped shoes. Everyone else, of course, had landed comfortably dry.

'You're going to get it, Wall,' she warned, lifting her feet out of the squelching muck.

Max was about to say more when she saw Steinberger becoming increasingly nervous. Each step he took became an exercise in finding the ground without stumbling or tripping over. He began talking to himself, softly, repeating something over and over. Max, Linden, and Irene realized he was practising saying hello. He brushed invisible lint from his suit and smoothed his eyebrows with his fingertips.

'I feel terrible about what's happened.' Irene wound her fingers into the knit of her jumper. 'Look what I've done to Steinberger.'

They watched as Steinberger spiked himself on a blackberry bush. The prickly branches caught on his jacket and the more he tried to unravel himself, the more tangled he became.

'It's because he's about to meet Frond,' Linden explained as he went to Steinberger's aid.

'Do you think so?' Irene's memory skipped back to the time in the canteen when Steinberger had tipped a whole pot of beetroot soup over himself after Frond had walked up to him and said hello. 'I guess it could be that, but I still feel bad. I'd never do anything to harm the Force.'

Max felt her back stiffen. She knew Irene felt low, but she also knew it was time for a good talking-to. 'Remember the time I received a parcel from Spy Force that had been bugged, and how it almost led to the infiltration of Spy Force? I felt really bad, too, but in the end it was Blue's malevolence that was to blame, not me, and no one blames you here either.'

Irene offered a small smile as she dragged her feet across the meandering, moss-covered path. Linden had managed to untangle Steinberger, who had briskly walked on ahead through the increasingly winding paths of the Plantorium.

'Max is right, Irene.' Linden smiled.

'Of course I am,' Max said in a softer voice. 'No one doubts your loyalty to the Force, Irene. Ask anyone around here and they'll tell you, Spy Force wouldn't be half the place it is without you.'

Irene's legs jellied at Max's comment. 'Thank you, Max. I . . .'

A panicked scream rustled through the Plantorium, followed by a muffled call for help.

Max and Linden spun towards each other. 'Steinberger!'

They ran past snaking plants, frothing ponds of piranhas, and plumes of prehistoric palms until they found him. Irene's hands flew to her mouth, Max's flew to her hips, and Linden stared. This was not what they were expecting to see. They all blinked to check that it was true.

Steinberger was being mauled by a giant plant.

Frond appeared from behind a jungle of huge fern leaves in her long red coat and beehive hairdo.

'What happened?' Worry rippled in her voice. 'Steinberger?'

'I'm afraid so,' Linden said.

A giant, bulbous sack at the end of a pond-dwelling plant was munching on Steinberger's head and shoulders, while the rest of his body poked unceremoniously into the air.

'What is it?' Max asked.

Frond pushed her rose-shaped glasses along her nose and fished through her lab coat for a small glass jar. 'It's a giant Utricularia vulgaris. An insectivorous plant more commonly known as a bladderwort.'

Linden's face screwed up. 'With a name like bladderwort, it can't be good.'

'Normally it's very good,' Frond added guiltily. 'But with all that's been going on, I forgot to feed it today. They're usually much smaller but we've been cultivating this one for years using a special fish fertilizer and it's just . . . blossomed.'

Frond opened the jar, which let out a pungent dead animal kind of smell.

Max held her nose. 'What's in that?'

'It's ground-up pieces of . . . actually, it's not important what it is. I explained the ingredients once before and it ended up in a bout of unexpected fainting.'

Frond waved the jar around the plant. Its long, skinny branches slowly uncoiled from Steinberger and he struggled free of its feeding bladder, which left whitish, dripping globs of plant gunk all over him.

Max and Linden helped Steinberger to stand. He pushed his soaking hair out of his face and tried to straighten his plant-globbed suit.

'I'm sorry, Steinby. Are you OK?' Frond winced as she surveyed his upper body.

The look of shock on Steinberger's face at almost being eaten by a giant bladderwort was replaced by a crushing look of awe.

'You're not hurt in any way?' Frond fed the bladderwort some bugs from her pocket. The plant immediately started to digest the bugs, far happier with those than the humany taste of Steinberger.

'I . . . it's . . . you.' He closed his mouth, deciding it was better that way.

'Why don't we go to my work area?' Frond suggested. 'We can take care of you there and I can look over the sample and tell you what I discover.'

At Frond's work area, Max and Linden helped Steinberger out of his soaking jacket and into one of Frond's lab coats. A bright red one with lady beetles on it.

'I . . . it's . . . you.'

'Thanks, Frond.' Max was keen to get beyond Steinberger's stuttering and on to Frond's testing. 'Irene has the bag the sample came in.'

Irene stepped nervously forward, as if she'd just been summoned to the principal's office. Frond smiled at her warmly. 'Thanks, Irene.'

Frond took the canvas bag and cut a sample small enough to fit on a microscope slide. She placed the slide under the lens and examined it closely. It looked like a completely normal mixture of spices and herbs, so she turned on the heat ray of the microscope. Now she could see traces of something more sinister.

'There,' she announced with a mixture of joy and trepidation. 'The blood parasite that causes the sleeping sickness.'

'That's excellent!' Max's shoulders fell in relief. 'Now you can work on creating the antidote Finch needs to wake the agents from their sleep.'

Frond went on staring into the lens of the microscope before slowly straightening up. 'I'm afraid it isn't that easy. From what Finch has told me, the parasite is carried by insects found in parts of Africa and South America. There's evidence here that this is the South American strain of the sickness, which is carried by the triatoma bug, also known as the kissing bug.'

Steinberger's small yelp at the mention of the word 'kissing' was met by a withering look from Max. 'Sorry,' he mumbled.

'Let me show you.' Frond turned to the computer beside her microscope and within seconds had an image of the bug on her screen. 'As you can see, the triatoma has a dark brown, flattened body with six reddish spots circling its wide abdomen. It has an elongated, cone-shaped head with elbowed antennae and a prominent beak.'

Linden remembered back to Finch's diagnosis. 'But I thought Finch said the disease is caused by the *bite* of the insects?'

'Normally it is, but in this case . . .' and here Frond's voice became edged with amazement, 'the sample has been infused with some kind of dormant or sleeping parasite. It's like nothing I've ever seen before.'

'So . . .' Irene was desperately trying to piece Frond's information together, 'when I added the sample to my food, the parasite woke up and put everyone to sleep?'

'That's how it appears.'

'Oh, it *was* all my fault.'

Linden looked firmly towards Irene. 'No. The fault is someone else's and Max and I are going to find out who. Right, Steinberger?'

'Ah . . . I . . . you.'

'Linden's right.' Frond offered Irene a smile that was like rich chocolate sauce but had the effect of ripping the floor from under Steinberger's feet. He stumbled against the desk, unsettling a stand of test tubes and beakers that his lanky arms scrambled to rescue.

Max was almost out of patience with Steinberger's lovesickness. She turned to Frond. 'So can you make the antidote?'

'I would need the pure form of the parasite to do that.'

'And all we need to do is get hold of the triatoma bug so you can extract the parasite?' Linden queried.

Max felt her shoulders tense again. 'Yeah, that's all.'

'At least we've narrowed down our search,' Frond said, trying to be optimistic.

Max wilted. 'Yeah, to the entire continent of South America.'

Just then a great crash echoed around them. Max turned around to see what damage Steinberger had done, but this time it wasn't him.

'Irene!' Linden ran to Irene's side and lifted her head from the cold floor. 'Irene, can you hear me?'

She didn't move.

'It must be the sleeping sickness.' Frond used her palm computer to contact Finch. 'I'll get someone here immediately to take her to the infirmary.'

Linden stroked Irene's pale face, desperate for her to wake up. 'Please be OK, Irene,' he said in a frightened whisper. He sniffed back a burning tear and stared helplessly at her limp body that looked as if all the life had been drained from her for ever.

CHAPTER 10
MISSION: TRIATOMA

Max and Linden walked down the corridor to Quimby's lab. They'd just left the infirmary, where Irene lay still and barely breathing, caught in the clutches of the sleeping sickness. Max stared at Linden as his feet thudded dully against the floor. She remembered the time in London when he had told her about his mother dying of cancer. He had the same look on his face now as he had then. She hated every second of that look and tried to think of something that would take it away, that would make him feel better, that would . . .

'It's OK, Max.'

'Sorry?' She hadn't expected him to say anything.

'I know you want to make me feel better about Irene, but you don't have to say anything. She's going to get better. I know it.'

How could he do that? How could Linden know exactly what she was thinking?

'Yeah. She is.' Once again Max had to put up with her mouth saying something dull when she wanted it to come up with something great.

Max and Linden had received a message from Harrison to get equipped by Quimby for their mission. They were going to the Amazon to find the triatoma bug.

'Ah, Max and Linden. We don't have much time. I've been given the brief by Harrison and I've assembled a range of devices that will be essential for your mission. This is the Hypnotron.' Quimby held out something that looked like a marble. 'Simply aim and activate it by squeezing. After thirty seconds your captive will be rendered hypnotized and ready to tell you anything you need to know. The hypnotic state ceases when you deactivate the device, or after a certain programmed amount of time. Now, don't forget,' Quimby surveyed the agents with a careful eye, 'you must not use the Hypnotron after your Spy Force business is complete. Spy Force equipment must only be used in the line of duty, otherwise we are in danger of becoming like the criminals we fight against. And then where's the difference?'

'No problemo.' Max tried to be chirpy for Linden's sake.

'Here we have the Mini Transporter Capsule, one for each of you.' She held out two matchbox-sized cubes. 'It is based on Francis, Ben, and Eleanor's Matter Transporter and is capable of transporting small, delicate objects through space. Place the triatoma bug in here as soon as you find it, enter the destination into the keypad on the side and off it will go. We have already lost precious time and any more time lost may have devastating consequences, so I recommend you place them in your pockets for easy access.'

Max and Linden did as they were told.

'I have also packed the Abseiler, which comes equipped with a safety harness and the new and improved miniature jet propulsion capsule for climbing over long distances. Where you are going is difficult terrain. You'll come across mountain peaks, impenetrable jungles, vast rivers and swamps. I've also added super-grip gloves. They're perfect for climbing mountains, scaling buildings, or clinging on to fast-moving objects.'

'What does this do?' Max held up a can that said 'Bug Repellent'.

'Repels bugs.' Quimby tried not to sound too obvious. 'A must to ensure you're not bitten when you find the triatoma. The repellent is completely non-toxic and is made from Frond's best plants in the Plantorium. As is this.' She reached for a small cloth bag sitting on the table. 'This is a bag of Animal Dispellers. It contains sachets of powders and sprays that will ward off most of the animals that you . . .' Quimby looked as if she was trying to find the right words, 'that you may come across.'

'What kind of animals?' Max asked warily.

'Oh, you know, the usual South American kind of animals, but I'm sure—'

'Such as?'

Quimby took a deep breath. 'Jaguars, pumas, snakes, alligators, piranhas—'

'Actually, Quimby,' Max interrupted, 'I think that's all I need to know for now.'

'These are super-tough covers for your palm computers. After Max's broke in the Nightmare Vortex, we knew we had to toughen them up.' Max and Linden took a transparent sleeve each and tucked their computers into them. 'They are waterproof, shockproof, and will withstand the most incredible pressure.'

When Quimby turned to outline the final articles in their packs, she momentarily lost her balance and fell against the bench.

'Quimby?' Linden sprang forward and caught her, but just as he did, he saw it. The terrible grey pallor of the sleeping sickness. 'You've got it, haven't you?'

There was a pause as the scientist got her breath back.

'I'm afraid I have.' Her voice was small.

'We've got to get you to Finch's infirmary.' Max

was frightened at how many agents had caught the illness.

'I've sent word,' she breathed. 'His assistants are on their way.'

Quimby turned away. Max didn't know what to say. As yet they only had a treatment from the Plantorium that could slow down the symptoms. No one knew if it was possible to create an antidote in time to stop the sleeping sickness from becoming fatal.

'We'll find the antidote, Quimby. Trust us.' Max offered her a confident look.

'Yeah, and besides,' Linden added, 'we can't let anything happen to you because then we won't have anyone to equip us for our missions.'

Max smiled. Even when Linden was scared, he still knew exactly what to say.

Quimby appreciated Max's and Linden's courage. Her smile was weak, worn down by the sickness and the grave spectre facing Spy Force. 'Finally, I've included your lasers, invisibility cream and antidote, and super-concentrate food capsules which have all the goodness of a wholesome, organic meal.'

Finch's assistants arrived and carefully placed Quimby on a stretcher, but before they carried her away, she looked at the two eager agents before her. 'Good luck and come back soon.'

Max and Linden watched as she was ferried down the corridor, both knowing that not only her fate but that of the whole of Spy Force rested entirely with them.

CHAPTER 11

THE EXPRESS WARDROBE AND A SHOCKING DISAPPEARANCE

As the express wardrobe to Harrison's office plummeted downwards, Max and Linden stabilized themselves by holding on to the rack of old clothes. The plunge unsettled their already nervous stomachs, but when the wardrobe came to a standstill, it also unsettled something else.

'Ouch!'

A storm of boaters, bowlers, pith helmets, and dust rained down on Max's head from a round leather hatbox.

'You'd think the top spy agency in the world could work out a more comfortable way to travel.'

'They need to be discreet,' said Linden.

'I'd like to know how I'm going to survive all this discreetness.'

Linden smiled and went to open the door, but stopped as they heard voices coming from the office, one commanding and serious, the other calm and attentive.

'Yes, sir . . . No, sir . . . You can count on me, sir.'

Max's brow creased. 'It's Agent Perfect. What's he doing here?' As she spoke, the dust from the hatbox nestled firmly into her nose, and an almighty sneeze took hold of her and flung her out of the wardrobe.

'Max. Linden,' the Chief of Spy Force began.

'Now that you're all here, I can brief you on Mission Triatoma. You remember Agent Suave, of course?'

Suave held his hand firmly out to Max.

'Of course,' Max gritted, and looked quickly at Harrison to avoid having to shake Suave's hand.

'Looks like I get to work with you sooner than I thought.' Suave's face glittered with a perfect smile. 'Don't worry, kids. We'll crack this case wide open.'

Linden flinched as he saw Max's face tense up. There were a few things that could make Max lose her temper and one of them was to call her 'kid'.

'Even though Suave is a new agent, his level of ability and skill is equal to that of some of the best agents in the Force.'

'Mr Harrison . . .' Max started to object, but Harrison held up his hand to stop her.

'Steinberger, activate the Shush Zone.'

Steinberger had replaced his lady beetle lab coat with a more subtle suit, and now that he was nowhere near Frond, he was back to his usual self. He ushered the agents into a tight circle behind Harrison's desk. He then pulled a small metal globe from his pocket and lifted it into the air, creating a sparkling green glowing curve around them that restricted what was said to their ears only.

Once the curve was complete, Harrison began.

'Sorry, Max. We have no idea how secure the agency is at this point, so we'll need to take every precaution. As I was saying before, Suave has passed all the required physical, moral, and intelligence tests, and after rigorous ID and Goodness checks, he came out smelling better than a spring flower show.'

Max was keen to stop talking about Suave and his smell. 'Do you think the sleeping sickness is related to the stolen Spy Force manual?' she asked.

Harrison flinched at the mention of the crime. 'I suspect it is, Max, but we're still working on it. Frond and Finch have given me their knickers . . . oh, sorry . . . their *briefs*, and their information about the sickness and the triatoma bug has been sent to your computers. I've also contacted Ben and Eleanor to let them know you've been placed on a mission and won't be home for a few days.'

'We're ready, sir,' Max replied.

'Absolutely, Mr Harrison,' Suave agreed in his overzealous way.

'All of you will be flown to a secret destination in Brazil in South America. We have pinpointed an area of the Amazon jungle where the concentration of the triatoma bug is at its highest. Steinberger will be your main contact for the mission. Keep him posted of all developments and he will take care of the operation from our end.'

'But, sir . . .' Max worded her next question carefully. 'Wouldn't it be better if we went on the mission with someone more experienced, like Agent Crane?'

Harrison smiled warmly, knowing Max's affection for Spy Force's top agent. 'Exactly what I was thinking. Steinberger, Alex and I have gone through what we know so far and after liaising with Finch and Frond, Alex is at present busy finalizing her plan of action. She will make the perfect mission feeder . . . oh dear . . . I mean *leader*.'

'Excellent!' Max yelled a little too excitedly. 'I mean, she will be a great leader, sir.'

'A wise decision, Mr Harrison,' Suave chimed in.

'Sleek is readying the Invisible Jet, which has been equipped with Quimby's Inflatable Foldaway Vehicles. The terrain you are about to enter is rugged and vast. Some of it has yet to even be ignored . . . make that *explored*. You will have time during the flight to read over all your material and become fully acquainted with how best to locate the bug and get it back to Spy Force. Alex will explain the mission details and Steinberger will be contactable twenty-four hours a day if you need his assistance.'

'Sir, couldn't we use the Time and Space Machine?' Max asked.

'Not this time, Max. Ben and Francis have advised us it doesn't have the weight capacity to transport the agents and equipment needed for this mission.' Harrison turned towards a miniature plasma screen positioned on his desk. 'Before you go, Frond has a few final words for you.'

Harrison called up Frond's direct videoline but a frown creased his forehead. He turned the screen to let the others see. 'She must have stepped away from her desk. I'll switch to a different angle.'

'Sir?' Steinberger lost his usual calm demeanour as Harrison moved the camera around the Plantorium by remote, but this time it wasn't Frond's presence that made him agitated, it was her absence.

'Hey, what's that?' As the camera angle shifted, Linden saw something on Frond's computer.

Harrison zoomed in. A note was stuck to the screen:

Your beloved Frond has gone.
Sorry there was no time for goodbyes.

'That's Frond's handwriting.' Steinberger's face went from crimson to white and back to crimson again as his eyes remained fixed on the screen.

'Are you sure?' Harrison stared at the fine handwriting.

'I'd put my life on it.'

'But why would Frond write her own kidnap note?' Max felt a weird chill at what they were seeing.

'This is much more serious than we thought.' Harrison seemed momentarily lost for words. 'Max, Linden, and Suave, you must complete your mission with Alex to find the triatoma bug and get back here as soon as you can. If what Finch and Frond say is true, we need that bug within seventy-two hours.'

Max opened her mouth to speak but was cut off by Suave. 'You can count on us, sir.'

'But, sir,' Linden said quietly, 'what about Frond?'

Harrison's eyelids wavered, as if they were being pulled shut and he was doing his best to resist.

'I . . . I . . .'

Linden and Max exchanged worried looks. 'Sir, are you OK?' Linden leant forward to see the chief's face more clearly.

'I must find her!' Steinberger cried out, his eyes still transfixed on the plasma screen, staring at the place Frond should have been.

Harrison moved to face Steinberger. 'Sorry, Steinberger, my decision has been made.' He tried to stifle a deep yawn. 'It is essential that you conduct the operation from here.'

Max and Linden could see Steinberger wasn't listening.

'Steinberger,' Harrison said with a warning ring in his voice, 'you have neither the in-field experience nor the stomach for this mission. And pardon me for saying so, but you've never been one for being in the middle of nature.' He paused, his eyelids drooping over his eyes. 'And I forbid you to put your life in danger by . . .'

And at that Harrison slumped into his chair, fast asleep.

From that moment, the bumbling Steinberger from the Plantorium was gone. He took out his palm computer and tapped at it decisively.

'Finch, Harrison is in his office and has the illness. We need medics here right away. Max,

Linden, Suave, and I are going in search of the triatoma bug and Frond, who has been kidnapped, no doubt for her expertise in the Plantorium. I know she briefed you on the antidote, so do everything you can to prepare until we return. Alex will remain here and direct the operation from the ground. And, Finch . . .' He stood taller for his James Bond-style sign-off, 'may the Force be with you.'

He shut down his computer then turned to Max and Linden with a steely look in his eyes that they'd never seen before. 'Let's go.'

Steinberger's determined step was cut short by a resounding thud that Max knew was the unmistakable ring of someone running into the Shush Zone. Steinberger rubbed his forehead. 'Once I deactivate this.'

He held out the silencing device and the green glowing curve of the Shush Zone disappeared.

Agent Suave stood in front of Steinberger, blocking his way to the wardrobe. 'I think we should follow Harrison's orders,' he challenged. 'If, as he pointed out, you have no in-field experience, it would be much better to . . .'

Steinberger inched his way towards Suave, standing as firm as his tall, gangly body would allow.

Max looked on, unable to tell if Suave's objection came from a genuine dislike of disobeying orders, or if he had some other reason he didn't want Steinberger on the mission.

'I am not only going on this mission,' Steinberger instructed with a quiet power that was very un-Steinberger-like, 'I'm heading it. If you have any doubts about my ability as a Spy Force agent, I suggest you take it up with Harrison when he wakes up, because by then we'll have rescued Frond, found the triatoma bug, and saved the lives of Spy Force agents from a potentially fatal illness.'

Max blinked as she tried to recognize the meek and sometimes bumbling Spy Force Administration Manager. Suave shifted uneasily in his over-pressed, immaculate suit. It was obvious he disagreed with Steinberger's plan, but it was also obvious he had no choice. 'Sure, Steinberger, it's just that . . .'

'Do you know where Frond is?' Linden saw something in Steinberger's eyes that told him he did.

'I'm almost certain of it.'

'Where is she?' Max stepped in front of a silenced Suave.

'It is widely known that Dr Frond is one of the

foremost professors of biology in the world. The powder that caused the sleeping sickness could only have been created by someone with a similar intelligence, but of an evil nature. It is no coincidence that the theft of the manual, Frond's disappearance, and the sickness occurred at the same time. I believe that when we find the triatoma, we will not only find Frond but the manual as well.'

Steinberger turned and walked into the wardrobe.

There were so many questions filling Max's and Linden's heads that for a second they couldn't move—until they saw Steinberger's face.

'There's no time to lose!' he commanded.

Max, Linden, and Suave hurried to the wardrobe, just in time for the door to close and hurl them directly into the beginning of their mission.

CHAPTER 12

A CALL FOR HELP AND A DEATHLY PLUNGE

'I've been told how you beat Blue without an ounce of Spy Force training.'

Suave had been trying to make conversation with Max as they waited in the VART beside the Invisible Jet, but with all that had been happening and the way his hair stared perfectly back at her, she wasn't keen to chat.

'That would have taken some nerve. I hear the guy's a real piece of work.'

Linden sat eating an apple and smiling as Max looked out for Steinberger, hoping he'd come back soon and save her from having to talk to this guy.

Finally Steinberger appeared at the end of the metal walkway. 'I've got it. Let's go.'

Steinberger held a pack he'd put together in Quimby's lab. He'd had to use Max's pack as a guide for the mission's devices since Quimby had been taken away sick. Now he strode towards them with purposeful steps, head high, knowing nothing would stop him.

Then he stopped. 'I hope I have enough handkerchiefs. That jungle's going to play havoc with my allergies.'

'Steinberger?' A voice came from behind. It was Alex. 'I won't let you head this mission.' Steinberger held his pack even more tightly.

'Alex, I have to go.'

'But it doesn't comply with Harrison's orders.'

'I agree,' Suave added.

Steinberger ignored Suave's comment and looked at Alex intently. 'I know Harrison wanted you on this mission, but with your knowledge of the Force and your natural leadership skills, I believe you will be better suited to commanding all aspects of the mission from here.'

Steinberger lowered his eyes a little.

'Plus, I believe I am the best person to find Frond.'

Max knew, no matter how hard they tried, they'd never be able to convince him to stay, not when Frond was in danger.

'We'll be fine, Alex, I promise. We'll complete this mission in record time, then everything can go back to normal.'

Alex had never gone against a directive from Harrison and Max could tell she was uncomfortable even with the idea, but Alex couldn't avoid the impenetrable determination etched into Steinberger's face.

'You will contact me the moment you're in trouble.'

Steinberger smiled. 'I will.'

'You will take no unnecessary risks . . .'

'None.'

'. . . and if the lives of any one of you is in danger you change tack or abort the mission immediately?'

'Change or abort. Absolutely.'

Alex stared at the Administration Manager. 'I'll send the mission plan to you immediately.'

'Thanks, Alex.' There was much more Steinberger wanted to say.

'Be careful.' It was barely a whisper from Alex before she leant in and kissed him on the cheek.

Steinberger blushed and turned quickly to enter the jet.

Max turned to Alex. 'Thank you.'

Alex gave a strained smile. 'Look after them, Max.'

Her chest exploded with pride.

'I will.'

Sleek's disembodied voice sounded over the intercom. 'Lady and gentlemen, this is your captain speaking. The Invisible Jet is ready for take-off. The Automatic People Sanitizer has been activated and is awaiting its first passengers.'

'I forgot about that.' Linden winced. The last time they had experienced the Sanitizer, it had felt as if his brains were being sucked out of his head.

'Do we really have to do this?' Max asked.

'It's an extra precaution,' Steinberger answered. 'Since the sleeping sickness has taken over, we can't afford to take any chances.'

The two agents squeezed through the entrance hatch of the Invisible Jet, which had been blocked by two balloon-like walls that led to a small white rubber room.

'You ready?' Max asked Linden.

'Only if you are.'

A blast of vacuum-like air sucked at their hair and clothes, whisking them round in circles and bouncing them off the soft walls. They were spun, twirled, and jostled before the suction stopped and they were spat out of the room and sent toppling into the jet.

'Sorry about that.' Steinberger was spat out behind them. He gained his balance, patted down his ruffled hair and made his way to his seat. 'I had it programmed to Super Clean.'

As Max and Linden took their seats, Max grinned at the entrance, waiting for Suave to blunder through. After a few seconds the agent stepped through as easily as if he was getting out of a car, his clothes intact and his hair still looking perfect. Max disliked him even more.

Steinberger pressed a button on his armrest and spoke to the jet's pilot. 'Ready to go, Sleek.'

The jet levitated and slowly made its way to the exit of the VART. It then thrust itself into action, forcing the agents into the backs of their seats as it began its high speed journey to the Amazon jungle.

Once they were at cruising altitude, Steinberger took out a small bag of herbal Plantorium medicines. He began swallowing pills, drinking measured pink liquids, and stirring bright green powders into various mugs of water.

'Steinberger?' Linden was curious.

'Allergies. The Plantorium staff put this together for me. It only takes little things to set me off if I'm not careful, so let's hope these tackle the Amazon, eh?'

When he was done, Steinberger put his pack away and looked intently at Alex's mission plan and accompanying maps of the Amazon on his palm computer.

Max watched as Steinberger busied himself with his notes and Linden opened his palm computer to read the mission briefing.

'Linden?' she whispered. 'We should say the pact.'

'We don't have to, Max. I know you don't like saying it.' He turned back to his computer screen.

It was true. In the past Max had thought holding hands and promising to take care of each other before a mission was embarrassing and way too sentimental, but this time she meant it. She wanted to let Linden know she would do everything she could to make sure he didn't get hurt. Or killed.

'Come on.' She tried to sound light as she grabbed his hands away from his computer keys. 'You know you can't live without it.'

Before Linden could object, Max started saying the pact, and for the first time, she remembered every word. 'If Linden M. Franklin should come to harm or get lost or be in danger in any way, I, Max Remy, will do everything I can to help him and bring him to safety.'

Linden was impressed and repeated his version of the pact.

Max sighed and let go of his hands. 'See? That wasn't so hard.'

Linden frowned, not sure where Max's change of heart for the pact had come from.

'What should we do first, Steinberger?'

'I think the first thing for us to do . . .'

Steinberger began, but he was interrupted by a message coming through on his palm computer. A broken image filled the screen, accompanied by the hiss and splatter of static. Underneath could be heard the fractured sounds of someone's voice.

'Who is it?' Max leant over.

Steinberger increased the volume and adjusted the settings. 'I'm not sure.' Then an icy jolt of recognition reverberated through Steinberger, Max, and Linden. The picture stabilized long enough for them to know it was Frond.

'Oh dear,' Steinberger breathed.

They played the message again to try and work out what Frond was saying. Max wrote down bits of information from the splintered message. 'Captured . . . triatoma . . . lab experiments . . .'

And then the last part before the transmission ended. 'Extreme danger . . .' The message suddenly became clear. 'Do not worry about me, please. The safety and security of Spy Force is much more important. My location is . . .'

Before she could say any more, the image shifted to a distorted angle, as if her palm computer had been thrown to the floor. The agents gazed helplessly as they heard the muffled sounds of Frond being forcibly taken away.

All four agents watched the crooked image until the leather boots of the attacker came back. One foot remained still as the other was lifted out of the image. Seconds later, with a violent snap, the picture became a cruel, desolate black.

Linden put his hand on Steinberger's back.

'We'll find Frond. We've got enough information to make a good start.'

'Yes, of course.' He tried to say more but his lips waved in an aimless shiver.

'Yeah. We'll find her before anything happens,' Max assured him.

Steinberger's mind filled with a skirmish of imaginings of what terrible things might be done to Frond, of what might be happening to her now.

But there was no time to dwell on these thoughts. At that moment the jet rolled forward, overbalancing into a slow but steady nosedive.

Max and Linden turned to each other. 'Sleek!'

Suave and Steinberger unbuckled their seatbelts and lurched their way to the front of the jet.

Max was having trouble with her belt, but when she did get it undone, the plane shifted sideways and she was flung headfirst into the wall of the jet.

'Max!' Linden turned from the door of the cockpit and climbed back to pull her up.

'Are you OK?'

'You mean apart from the fact that we're plummeting to our deaths?'

'Good,' Linden smiled. 'You're fine.'

They pushed through the door into the cabin and saw Steinberger pulling an unconscious Sleek into the co-pilot's seat and strapping him in. Next to them, Suave was at the flight controls. 'We'll have to land where we can,' he announced to no one in particular.

'You know how to fly this thing?' Linden yelled above the droning fall of the jet.

'A little,' Suave answered calmly, as he tried to lift the jet from its spiralling fall. 'Sleek's been giving me lessons.'

'You just happen to know how to . . . Aaaah!'

Max was flung to the floor as the sharply descending plane hit the top of a cluster of trees, damaging one of the engines. Suave tried to pull the plane up.

'It's no good. We need more power. We'll have to make an emergency landing.'

Linden clung to the back of the pilot's seat and Max tried to stand up, but her efforts were interrupted by a food hatch that flung open, knocking her out and sprinkling her with a powdery mixture of coffee and sugar.

'I suggest you all strap yourselves in,' Suave said. 'This may not be one of the smoothest landings you'll ever have.'

Steinberger and Linden managed to get Max to a seat and strap her in before doing the same themselves.

As Linden gripped his hand rest, he concentrated on watching Suave's sure grip on the controls and his face sculpted with determination.

The window of the jet filled with the deep green and brown tangle of the jungle coming closer and closer. Suave craned his head to find a clearing to land in and realized there was none. He tried to slow the jet down as much as he could to make the landing. It wasn't ideal, but it was the only choice they had.

'Hold on!' he yelled, barely turning his head, as the jet made its wayward descent into the heart of the Amazon jungle.

CHAPTER 13

A RUDE AWAKENING AND AN ALMOST FATAL STEP

Agent Max Remy ran along the damp stone tunnels that snaked their way deep beneath the city of Paris. Her shoes splashed through the algae-strewn pools of water that dribbled beneath the hum and splendour of the majestic city.

She was pursuing the dreaded and devious Sir Snivel Snodbottom, France's most fraudulent gangster, who had used his hypnotic charms to seduce the richest and most powerful of French citizens into handing over vast sums of expensive jewels, antiques, and artwork.

His latest scam was taking place in the Louvre, one of the world's most famous art museums. Snivel had charmed the head curator of the museum into handing over some of its most valuable works, but just as the deal was about to be done, Max lowered herself through a manhole into the curator's grand art-filled office.

'Your thieving days are over, Snivel!' But before Max could move any further, Snivel turned and ran through a concealed exit behind him.

Max ran after him through ornate corridors and rooms filled with huge portraits and elegant sculptures of Greek goddesses under long, ornately carved domed ceilings. The museum had been closed for hours, and the low level lights outlined a path for Snivel to a secret trapdoor that led him down to the city's sewers.

Max followed quickly after him, opening the trapdoor and landing in a squelching stream of water below.

The low lights of the tunnel caught the edges of Snivel's weaselly frame as he splashed through the watery passage like a scurrying rat. The sound of a thousand drips echoed around the coarse stone walls, which swept into a sudden curve, and Snivel disappeared from Max's sight.

'You won't get away that easily,' she breathed.

As she swung around the ominous corner, her feet slid to a precarious stop, only centimetres from the frothing edge of a long, cascading fall.

Max looked about her, trying to find a sign of Snivel in the wide pool that opened out below her. But what she saw, through the flickering shadows and deafening wash of water, was something that gripped her heart.

Linden was suspended above the pool in a giant web, as if caught by a spider.

'I'm not sure I'm ready for my thieving days to be over, Ms Remy.' Snivel's voice rose above the watery din, but he was nowhere to be seen. 'So while I get back to business, I will leave you to work out how to save your little friend.'

Each fear-filled breath scratched at Max's throat as she searched for a way to save Linden. All around her, similar stony passages ended in the same abrupt fall.

'Linden?'

He didn't answer, his body lightly buffeted by the swirling winds of the cavern.

'Oh, wait, there's one more thing I almost forgot to do.'

From out of the blackness shot a fiery arrow. It made a direct hit into the outer thread of Linden's web. Terror rose in Max like a rising wave of nausea, as she watched what happened next.

The small flame latched onto the rope like a burning fuse, making its way around the outer layer of the web, sending a disintegrating wisp of ash into the churning water below.

'Bye-bye, kids.' Snivel's laugh rang out loudly before receding into the murky darkness.

Max watched as the flame wound its way closer and closer to Linden, burning the only thing between him and certain death. She had to save him. She had to try and reach him before—

* * *

'Aaaah!' Max opened her eyes to see the creeping legs of a giant spider crawling over her hand. She shook the eight-legged animal into the air and it landed with a small bounce on the floor of the jet.

'A tarantula. Excellent! I never thought I'd see one in the wild.'

Linden was sitting in the chair next to Max, wide-eyed at their hairy, slow-moving visitor.

'That thing is a tarantula? I could have been killed!'

Killed . . . Linden's fall, Max thought sadly. When would these nightmares stop?

Linden kept his eyes fixed on the spider as it made its way to the broken hatch of the jet. 'They might give you a painful bite but most of them aren't deadly.'

'That makes me feel much better.' Max rubbed her aching head and felt a small lump where she'd been struck by the food hatch.

The spider sprang from the jet and it was then that Linden noticed the dense greenery outside. 'I guess we're here. The Amazon jungle.'

After the jet had made its unexpected and invisible landing, there'd been a scattering of birds, animals, and insects, but after a few minutes they'd crept back to see who their uninvited guests were.

Max swiped angrily at a mosquito that was circling her head, but in her stupor, she missed the mosquito and struck her ear instead. 'Ow!'

She tried to remember what had happened.

The flight. The plunge. Then the last thing she remembered.

The smug face of Suave at the controls just before everything went black.

'Could have been smoother, but otherwise not a bad landing for a beginner.' Linden made his announcement in his usual unruffled way.

Max shooed away another mosquito and smiled. Seeing Linden's wide grin beneath his hurricaned hair drove away her storm-clouding bad mood.

She went to stand but was pulled back by her seatbelt.

'Are you OK?' asked Linden.

'For someone who was almost flown to their death, I'm fine.'

Max was pulling roughly at the belt that was strangling her when they heard a voice behind them.

'Frond . . . we're coming. Everything will be all right.' A mumbled pledge wormed its way out of Steinberger's lips.

'Looks like Steinberger's OK.' Linden undid his seatbelt and stood over the Administration Manager, wiping Steinberger's face with his hanky. The day had only just begun but the heat was starting to settle on their skin in waves.

'Hope that's clean.' Max raised an eyebrow in mock disgust.

'It's clean,' Linden assured her.

Steinberger opened his eyes. 'Better be.'

'I'll guarantee it!' It was unusual to hear Steinberger joke and Linden enjoyed every bit of it. 'Nice to have you back.'

Steinberger offered an uneasy smile, then remembered something and quickly reached into his pocket. His face calmed when he saw that Quimby's transparent cover had protected his palm computer, and Frond's message, from damage.

'She'll be OK.' Linden gave him a crooked smile.

'Yes, of course she will.'

A raised voice then came down the aisle from the front of the crashed jet.

'We're losing altitude! I'm employing reverse thrust! Hold on, everyone.'

The three agents turned and saw the door of the cockpit had been wrenched off one of its hinges and was hanging limply across the entrance. Light slithered its way through the thin crooked wedge, revealing Suave manipulating the air with his eyes closed, pushing imaginary buttons and knobs trying to control the plane.

'Looks like Suave's getting an instant replay,' Linden winced. 'Going through that crash once was enough for me. We'd better wake him up.'

Max slapped at her leg as another mosquito bit through her trousers in a stinging jab.

'What about Sleek?' Steinberger asked as he struggled to his feet.

'I'll check on him too.'

Linden led the way towards the cockpit, pushed aside the broken door and saw Sleek sitting in the co-pilot's seat in a limp, folded heap. Steinberger gently shook Suave, whose eyes shot open in a confused daze until he saw Sleek. 'Is he OK?'

Linden reached out and took Sleek's wrist, trying to find a pulse. He'd studied first aid at the Country Firemen's Association in Mindawarra and was usually good at finding the pulse first go, but now he had to move his fingers around the wrist, searching for the surging of blood that would show Sleek was alive. Finally he found it.

'It's faint,' he told the others. 'But it's there.'

Max's eyes were fixed on something else. 'He has the colour of the sleeping sickness in his face.'

She was right. Steinberger immediately reached into his pack and took out a needle. It was Frond's Plantorium medicine Finch had given him in case any of them should fall victim to the sickness. He rolled up Sleek's sleeve and rubbed a small circle of skin with antiseptic before holding the syringe up high to ensure it was ready. As he watched the thin length of the needle and the tube of fluid about to be splurted into the vein, Steinberger's face went pale and he began to sway.

'I can do that.' Linden took the needle gently from the woozy-looking Steinberger. 'Maybe it'd be best if you looked away.' Steinberger gratefully did as he was told as Linden guided the needle into Sleek's arm.

'Thanks.' Steinberger took a deep breath. 'I usually pass out at the sight of those things. He'll need this as well.'

Steinberger took a mini-respirator from his pack and, stretching the plastic strap around Sleek's head, fixed an oxygen mask to his face.

'This will assist his lungs to function during the sickness.' Steinberger held his forehead, a niggling headache working away in his head. 'He should be all right. For a while.'

He looked towards Suave. 'You saved our lives. Thank you.'

The two men shook hands. It was all that needed to be said.

At least according to them.

'Yeah, and lucky we had such thick forest to cushion our fall or we'd all be smears of gooey Spy Force mush by now.'

'Max, my stomach is still recovering from the fall . . . could you be less descriptive, please?' Linden held his queasy stomach, trying to convince it not to go anywhere.

'Sorry about that,' Suave apologized.

But Steinberger was right. They had been almost killed, and it had been Suave who had saved them.

Max was more shaken by the jet's plummet than she wanted to admit. She was scared by what had happened to Sleek. With the importance of their mission, she knew they couldn't afford to lose anyone else.

Suddenly she felt the thick heat of the jungle that had moved in around them. 'I think I need some air.'

She made her way to the broken hatch the tarantula had jumped from a few minutes before.

'Aaaahh!'

Max made a grab for the hatch as she stepped out into nothingness, noticing too late that the jet had landed in the thick canopy of the jungle, which was acting like an overgrown hammock. Max clung to the broken door, her legs scissoring through the air as her mind became strangled with panic at the sight of the dizzying drop to the forest floor.

'Max!' Linden sprang forward to save her. 'Hold on!' Standing on the edge of the doorway, he reached into his pack for his Abseiler and quickly fixed it around himself, attaching the super-grip fibres to the inside of the plane.

As the device took hold, Max's eyes drifted back in her head. A wave of numbness flooded over her. Her fingers loosened from the door and she fell.

CHAPTER 14

A SUSPICIOUS MUFFIN AND AN ATTACK OF NERVES

Linden leapt out of the plane like a high diver at the Olympics and within seconds grabbed hold of Max as she began her freefall to a certain death.

'Gotcha!' he whispered to himself as they swung Tarzan-style through the corridor of trees. Allowing for the rope's swing to slow a little, Linden slowly retracted the Abseiler to pull them both to safety.

Back inside the jet, Max's life was still flashing through her mind as she opened her eyes to see Suave leaning over her slapping her cheek. Steinberger and Linden were fanning her with the bottom of their shirts. They were all asking if she was OK, but their voices wavered around her in pieces as if someone was turning the volume up and down.

Something about what was happening became annoyingly clear.

'You can stop hitting me now.'

Suave stopped and Linden sighed in relief. 'She's OK.'

'Well done, Linden.' Steinberger smiled at Max. 'You frightened us for a minute there. Promise me you'll be more careful in future. We're not ready to say goodbye to you yet.'

Linden and Suave laughed quietly at

Steinberger's joke, but Max's face burned a glowing puce. She was grateful her life hadn't ended in a squelching pile in the middle of the Amazon jungle. She just wished she could tone down the near-death experiences she gave herself.

As Steinberger prepared to announce their next step, the jet lurched downwards in a stomach-churning creak. Insects and birds scattered again in a shrieking and panicked squall.

When Steinberger had recovered enough of his senses to be coherent, he gave his orders in a clear, precise stream.

'Max and Linden, I need you to use your Abseilers and get down to the ground. I'll contact Alex and tell her what has happened, and Suave, I need you to assess the damage to the engine and calculate how safe the jet is in these treetops.'

'Right away.' Suave leapt into action like a spring-loaded frog.

Max took her Abseiler from her pack, also eager to follow orders, until she looked outside the jet. She swooned again when she saw the distance to the ground.

'Best thing is to not look down.' Linden knew about Max's fear of heights and began calmly readjusting the Abseiler harness around his waist.

'The trick is to concentrate on every step. Ready?'

'Yep,' she answered, even though her real answer was no.

Linden waited until Max had prepared her Abseiler.

'Looks like we're set, then.'

The way he looked at her instantly made Max feel safe, as if he'd somehow moved the jet closer to the ground. They both climbed outside the craft and began their slow descent. Step by step, Max concentrated just as Linden had said, until they reached the ground and fell in a relieved slump against a tree.

'I told you it'd be OK.' Max gave Linden a cheeky smile, enjoying the feel of solid ground beneath her. 'Bug repellent?'

They reached into their packs and applied the spray to ward off the squadron of bugs droning around them. Linden then held out a sesame seed bar he'd brought from home. 'Want some?'

No matter where they were, Linden always seemed to be able to pull food from some part of his clothes.

Max took the bar. 'Thanks.' She hadn't eaten since they'd left Mindawarra and her stomach was letting her know it. 'Maybe we should take one of our meal capsules.'

'I've already done that,' Linden replied. 'Doesn't quite have the same kick as biting into a real piece of food.'

'You're right.' Max broke the bar in half, then remembered something.

'How do you know about giving injections?'

Linden took his half of the bar. 'I had to give them to Mum when she was really sick.'

Max watched a mosquito as it buzzed around trying to find some bare skin to bite. 'That must have been hard.'

'A bit. Dad did it at first but as Mum got even more sick, I could see it was starting to get to him, so I took over.'

Linden leant back against the tree and bit into his bar.

Max sat turning hers in her hands, knowing exactly what she wanted to say but feeling as if someone had wired her jaws together. Linden chewed and sighed and took in their new jungle surroundings. Max sat and stared as the bar melted on to her fingers.

Then she just burst out with it.

'Thanks for saving my life before, I'm sorry I'm

such a klutz, I know I should be more careful but I just can't seem to help it, all you've ever done is be there for me and all I do is keep messing things up and opening my big mouth and getting us into trouble and even . . .' She had to say it, 'even getting you killed.'

She'd done it. She'd finally said it. It left her mouth dry and her knotted stomach slightly queasy.

Linden finished his mouthful. 'Is that what all your nightmares have been about?' he asked softly.

Max lowered her head as images from the dreams crowded into her mind. 'Yep. In each one you're stuck somewhere high and then you fall and I can't save you.'

She blinked to stop the tears that were threatening to fall, a hard lump pressed against the back of her throat.

'I'm so sorry, Linden.' She bit her lip.

'But, Max, you've forgotten one thing. You didn't let me fall. You caught me, remember?'

'But the first time I didn't. I just watched it happen.'

'Well, as far as I'm concerned, it's the second time that counts, because that's the one that means I'm still your spy partner.'

Max sniffed a small laugh.

'And me saving you back there was just returning the favour. Mum always said one good turn deserves another. I was just doing what Mum said.'

Max's sick stomach feeling melted away.

'And I'll tell you another thing, Max Remy.' He was starting to get fired up. 'If you hadn't saved me from the Nightmare Vortex, I'd still be trapped in one of Blue's most evil inventions,* spending the rest of my life facing the things that scare me most. The day you first came to Mindawarra, my life jumped to a whole new level, and with all that's happened since then, I wouldn't change one thing, especially the part about knowing you.'

Max stared. She'd never seen Linden so animated. And then, a little more calmly, he said, 'That Suave is pretty good.'

She followed Linden's gaze up the tree. Suave lay between two branches as if he was reclining on a deckchair, pointing his torch into the belly of the jet's engine.

Max smiled. Linden saved people's lives as easily as most other kids rode bikes. No matter who

*See *Max Remy Spy Force: The Nightmare Vortex*

she'd meet for the rest of her life, she knew Linden would be one of the best.

And he was right, she admitted to herself, Suave was pretty good.

Steinberger, on the other hand, was nestling in his Abseiler harness, clinging desperately to the nearest branch, handing Suave tools as he needed them.

'How do you think Steinberger's going to like his first mission?' Linden asked.

'It's going to be a steep learning curve,' Max grimaced.

'Hopefully one that won't fall on him and kill him. Watch out!' Linden grabbed Max as a wrench fell only metres from them. 'Or us.'

'Sorry,' Steinberger called down.

Linden smiled slyly. 'I bet on this mission he finally admits what he feels about Frond.'

'There's no way! He's been holding back for years.'

'We'll see,' Linden smiled. 'How's your mum's wedding going?'

Max was suddenly pulled from their mission smack bang into the middle of the freak-show of life back at home. 'It's like this huge tornado has landed in our house and won't go away. It's always full of designers, cake makers, and dress fitters and the phone has been ringing so much that any minute now it's going to self-combust from overuse.'

'So everything's pretty normal, then?'

Max laughed. 'Yeah, I guess so.'

Now that the initial impact of the crash had passed, a slowly increasing racket of animal and insect noise was firing up all around them. Max and Linden weren't that fazed by the whistles, screeches, hisses, and hoots, and when Linden noticed a giant moth land on his shirt, he gently picked it off and nestled it onto the bark of the tree.

There was something far more dangerous to be worried about: Steinberger was starting to navigate his ungainly way down with his Abseiler.

'I think we better stand for this,' Linden warned Max.

They watched as he stood on the edge of the jet's door, ready to abseil down. His shoulders lifted in a confidence-building breath, but just as he jumped, a giant butterfly flapped past his face, and his careful descent became a speedy slide all the way to the ground.

'Well done, Steinberger,' Linden said proudly.

'The Spy Force Gym Team's going to be calling you up when they hear about this.'

Steinberger gulped great chunks of air and smiled when he realized he was still alive. 'Oh, come now.' He leant on a tree for support, but felt something strange. It was the spindly legs of a stick insect as it moved gingerly onto his fingers. He pulled his hand from the tree as if it was on fire and shook it vigorously, then tucked it safely into a pocket.

Meanwhile, Suave had finished his work, packed his tool bag, and made his way down with his Abseiler, landing firmly on the ground like a trapeze artist finishing a routine on the high wire.

'How does it look?' Steinberger swished bugs from his face and brushed their crawling droves from his clothes.

'She's too damaged to fly. I'm not sure if I can fix her, but I can give it a shot.'

'There's no time.' Steinberger looked at his watch. 'We must get on with the mission immediately. How stable do you think she is?'

'After that last jolt, she's settled pretty firmly into some solid branches. I've added some Abseiler rope for extra protection.'

'What about Sleek?' Linden wasn't sure leaving

the sick pilot behind was a good idea. Even if the jet was stable, there were enough animal noises around them to suggest it might not be so safe to be alone in the jungle.

'With Frond's medicine and Finch's mini-respirator, he should be fine for at least the next forty-eight hours. I also added some Bug Repellent to him and spread Animal Dispeller sachets all around him,' Suave said.

Max looked at Agent Perfect and wondered if he ever got bored with being such a hero.

'What if we can't find our way back to the plane?' she asked.

'We all have our palm computers with us, including Sleek.' Steinberger took out his. 'So we will know where the jet is using his locator.'

Thankfully all the computers had survived the bumpy landing.

'What did Alex say?' Max asked.

'She took a reading of our area and confirmed we're in the heart of triatoma territory. She's also organizing a transport carrier called the Goliath to make its way here. It will load the Invisible Jet into its hold and wait for us here until our mission is complete.'

His voice had filled with the importance of

what he'd just said, but another butterfly flew at him and he collapsed into a hand-waving mess.

'Maybe some of this will help?' Max offered him her Bug Repellent.

As both Steinberger and Suave applied their repellent, the noise and movement of the jungle increased. Max started imagining monkeys, snakes, lizards, and spiders, all of which seemed to be hidden only centimetres away. Branches moved suddenly above them, bushes rattled beside them, and the flapping of giant wings whomped somewhere in the jungle behind them.

Steinberger was the least easy with their surroundings. He'd rarely been outside England, and during his years of employment with Spy Force he'd hardly left London. His brow was speckled with sweat at the heat and the thought of the animals around them. The repellent seemed to calm him down, as it immediately sent insects and bugs away, but when he looked down, the colour fell from his face like a leaking thermometer.

'I . . . Is that . . . ? Oh dear.'

A thick green snake slid across his shoe.

Max and Linden got ready to catch what they thought would be a fainting Steinberger until what happened next.

Another message came through on his palm computer.

He took out the bleeping device and stared at its miniature screen.

'Who's it from?' Linden studied Steinberger's face, hoping the news wasn't bad.

'It's Frond.'

The snake slithered away without Steinberger giving it another thought.

'How's she getting her message through? It looked like her palm computer had been crushed.' Max frowned as a wide smile filled Steinberger's face.

'Clever girl,' he whispered, almost to himself. 'She's using her video watch. It's a new design of Quimby's. She must have given it to Frond to test out. The watch is so small that even under close scrutiny it still looks like a simple watch, but it is capable of transmitting messages across the world from almost any location with perfect clarity.'

Frond's message contained a reference to a map, which Suave quickly located on his palm computer. She then gave the specific longitude and latitude points of where she was.

'Can you work that out, Suave?'

'Ten four,' he snapped.

While Suave worked out Frond's exact location, Steinberger listened to the rest of the message. Frond explained that she was being held captive in a mansion where a lab was experimenting with stolen local plants and recipes that were hundreds of years old to create potions and serums. They were also conducting experiments using the triatoma bug. The message then ended with one simple plea.

'Take care, all of you.'

Her last sentence lingered in the air. Steinberger ran a finger across his computer where Frond's face had just disappeared. 'So she is here.'

Suave interrupted Steinberger's musing with the location.

'Got it! Should be only a few hours from here.'

'Let's go,' said Steinberger, once again in charge of his feelings. 'We must find Frond and gather the triatoma bug fast. Agents' lives depend on us getting back to Spy Force as soon as we can.'

They prepared to leave, but as Suave swung his pack onto his shoulders, a half-eaten muffin flew into the air and fell with a clump on the ground nearby.

Steinberger, Max, and Linden stared. First at the muffin, then at Suave.

'That's one of Irene's. I'd know it anywhere.' Linden's mouth hung slightly open at the sight of the golden and fluffy mango treat. Even though he knew it was dangerous to eat, possibly even fatal, it took all his self-control not to reach out and devour it in one large, delicious gulp.

Max was immediately suspicious. 'How did this get into your bag?'

'I . . . I . . .' Suave tugged at the collar on his shirt. The humidity was sticking to his skin like a sheet of clingfilm.

'Well, Suave?' Steinberger asked.

'During my final tour of Spy Force, I was shown Irene's kitchen and offered one of these muffins. Normally I don't touch sweet things, but when I was told how delicious they were I took one for later.' He looked guiltily at the muffin as it lay at his feet.

'Have you eaten some of this?' Steinberger knew they couldn't afford any of them becoming sick.

'No! No. I haven't,' he answered all too quickly.

The story fell into place for Max. 'But Sleek has. That's why he passed out.'

Suave just stared at them.

Max was about to let him have it, when

Steinberger interrupted her. 'Let's keep moving.'

'But, Steinberger . . .'

'Max. It's time to move on,' he said decisively.

'Max is right to be suspicious, Steinberger,' admitted Suave. 'That's how it looks.'

He was playing innocent and Max could see right through it.

'Everyone here is well and we have a mission to complete,' Steinberger said. 'And there's nothing more to be said.'

'Yes, there is,' insisted Max. 'At the start, I caught him staring at me like he was up to something. And he did arrive at Spy Force at exactly the same time as the sleeping powder. Now we have a half-eaten muffin and a pilot in a coma!'

Max eyed Suave, a small triumphant smile tickling the corner of her lips, but that was wiped away by what Steinberger said next.

'Show her, Suave.'

Suave undid the buttons of his shirt to reveal a rectangular metallic device stuck to his chest. From this, three thin cords networked across his skin and ended in small white sticking plasters.

Max stared at the set-up. 'What's that?'

'It's a portable lie detector,' Steinberger explained. 'The moment Suave even slightly deviates from the truth, it sets off a high-pitched whistle. It is now standard procedure that all agents wear them for a specified period after beginning work at the Force. Suave was told about this and instantly agreed. And now, I suggest we get back to the mission.'

He waited to see if Max had any other objections before turning on his heel and walking into the jungle.

Max flicked away a fly and clenched her lips, desperately wanting to argue. It was obvious Suave was up to something, even if the lie detector hadn't squealed yet, and before the mission was over she was going to find out what.

They moved through the jungle, following Suave's directions to Frond's location. Because they'd left Spy Force in a hurry, there had been no time for Steinberger to find appropriate clothes, and his regular business shoes were having a hard time negotiating the ragged floor of the Amazon. The path they were on was knotted with thick twisting roots slithering from the base of trees that stretched high overhead into the thick jungle roof. Steinberger's suit was continuously tugged at by branches and palms and thorny bushes. Max watched as he wiped his brow again. She knew how he felt. The heat was flooding all around them as if they were walking through a heated pool. Steinberger tripped again and fell forward into a spiky bush, then untangled himself without complaint. Even though she disagreed with him about Suave, Max liked Steinberger more at that moment than she ever had.

'Oh, dear.' Steinberger stepped onto a large mossy rock and slid down the other side, only staying upright with the help of a thick vine strung between two trees. Almost immediately, the screeching of monkeys filtered down from the overlapping layers of leaves. Rustling branches swayed above them, as if the treetops had come to life.

The ground beneath their feet was damp and cluttered with jungle debris: leaves, twigs, rotten logs, and a damp mulching cover that let loose the smell of rich black earth at each step.

Holding up the rear in order to keep an eye on Suave, Max stared at each sodden step of her now jungle-stained shoes, not noticing the others duck beneath an enormous lattice-like spiderweb.

'Max! Watch out!' Suave was too late. Max became tangled in the sticky trap which instantly filled with a swarm of scuttling spiders heading straight towards her.

'Aaaah!'

She spun into an arm-waving frenzy, brushing the spiders off her and trying to get out of their silken lair.

Steinberger stared on helplessly, gripped by an ironbound arachnophobia, as Linden and Suave leapt forward to help de-spider Max. They picked off the creatures as they spread over Max like a hairy coat that had come to life, crawling inside her shirt, onto her neck, and into her hair.

Finally, after more screaming and an accidental slap in the head to Suave by a panicked Max, Linden plucked the last of the spiders from her.

'I think that's the last,' he sighed in relief. 'Now you're back to normal.'

Max's hair stuck out at all angles in a mangled crush. She was embarrassed that she'd lost it so badly, and as Suave opened his mouth to say something, she quickly interrupted.

'Better keep moving.'

She'd spent enough time making a fool of herself in front of Suave, so she moved behind Steinberger as they made their way further into the jungle.

The agents pushed aside giant palm leaves, tree branches, and fern fronds like multiple layers of curtains. After what felt like hours, they pushed through another tangle of foliage and stared silently at what stood before them.

'Any suggestions?' Linden asked.

The dense and cluttered jungle had fallen away into a deep ravine, as if an ancient earthquake had ripped the Amazon in two. A thin layer of ghostly cloud hovered just out of reach, buffeted by a strong wind. The two jagged cliff edges had been joined by a long woven rope bridge, with misshapen and gnarled planks sewn in at uneven intervals. The problem was, the bridge had collapsed and was now clattering sadly against the cliff below them like a torn sail on a boat.

'Give us a hand, Linden.' Suave knelt at the cliff edge and grasped at the piece of rope.

'I can help too,' Max said indignantly.

'Of course.'

But as she knelt, she kicked a rock over the edge, and once again felt her mind go into rapid meltdown at how high they were. Max clutched at a sturdy tree root and concentrated on breathing as Suave and Linden pulled the rope bridge up and laid it on the ground before them. Suave looked closely at the frayed ends and frowned.

'This rope has been cut in the last twenty-four hours.'

Max moved slowly away from the edge. 'Yeah, right. And how can you tell that?'

Suave missed the cynicism and began to explain.

'The broken threads of the rope have been cleanly separated. If they'd been worn away the edges would be much more random and frayed. Also, there is a big difference between the newly severed threads and the rest of the rope that's been at the mercy of the elements. It's a guess, but I'd say twenty-four hours tops.'

Linden was impressed. 'Very clever.'

'Remarkable,' Steinberger added.

'Just your basic spy training,' Suave said modestly.

Max was keen to leave the chasm that was threatening every second to pull her in. 'Looks like we have to find somewhere else to cross.'

Suave put down his bag. 'Actually, Max, there's no time. My guess is, this broken bridge means someone knows we're here and is trying to stop us completing our mission. It's time for the Abseiler.'

Suave began casually taking out his gear, as if he was getting ready for soccer training.

'Right you are.' Steinberger followed suit with uneasy but determined moves.

‘Please tell me I heard that conversation incorrectly,’ Max pleaded with Linden.

‘I’ll help you with your Abseiler if you like,’ was all he could offer.

‘Why can’t we just use the Heliocraft?’

Suave looked into the ravine as a sudden burst of wind soared upwards. ‘I can’t guarantee that wind won’t overbalance the craft. The Abseiler’s super-grip fibres, on the other hand, could withstand a wind twice as strong.’

Max sighed, knowing she had no choice.

Linden watched as Steinberger prepared his Abseiler and knew Steinberger’s enthusiasm was a flimsy cover for an otherwise terrified man.

‘I’ll go first and make sure the other cliff edge is secure. When I give the all-clear, you each follow using my Abseiler rope.’ Suave finished tightening his harness around his chest and, using Quimby’s new and improved jet-propulsion function, sent the super-grip device hurtling towards the other cliff face.

Attaching the harness strap to the rope and wearing his super-grip gloves, Suave swung his way across the ravine like an action figure that had come to life.

Linden prepared for his turn and whispered to

a pale Max, 'You'll be fine. Pretend it's just the monkey bars at school . . . and don't look down.' He manoeuvred his way along the super-grip rope and effortlessly followed Suave's example.

Max felt the same shiver of fear that had cemented her to the ledge of the virtual cascades in Spy Training Class with Alex, making her unable to move.* This time, however, the plunging chasm below her was real and promised a definite and painful death if she failed. She took a deep breath and smiled at an equally nervous Steinberger before doing exactly as Linden had told her.

'Don't look down. Concentrate on each move.' Her harness firmly fixed to the rope, Max raised one hand and took a firm grip. 'Concentrate, Max.' Both gloved hands now held onto the rope. 'Don't look down. Remain calm,' she coached. 'Concentrate on your first . . .'

'Come on, Max. You can do it.'

Suave's call from the other cliff top made her look up.

Then down.

'Aaaahh!'

She overreached and began her high-wire

*See *Max Remy Spy Force: Spy Force Revealed*

climb with her breath stuck in her lungs and her heart threatening to leap out of her mouth.

'Breathe . . . concen . . . don't look . . . calm,' she stammered.

'Come on, Max,' Linden whispered. 'Stay calm.'

As if Max had heard Linden's wish, she regained her calm and, grip by grip, slowly made her way to the other side.

Suave and Linden pulled her in when she reached the rocky edge.

'Well done, Max,' Suave congratulated her.

'Yeah,' grumbled Max. 'Thanks for your help.'

It was Steinberger's turn. Steinberger was a brilliant Administration Manager but nothing back at his desk at Spy Force had prepared him for this. He'd watched the others and pepped himself up with encouraging slogans. 'You can do it, Steinberger. There's nothing to it. What could possibly go wrong?'

As he stepped up to the edge of the cliff, his hands sweating inside his super-grip gloves, the dry dirt gave way beneath his shoes and he slipped forward. His eyes widened at the gaping pit beneath him as his feet desperately scrambled to cling to solid ground.

'Steinberger!'

Max's call drew his eyes up. He saw her anxious face, willing him not to fall.

But it was too late. His hands reached for something to save him—the rope, a branch, a vine—but they were all out of reach.

His harnessed and gangly body, overdressed in his suit and tie, tipped over the edge. Max, Linden, and Suave watched as if it were happening in slow motion, their collective minds refusing to believe what they were seeing. They all gasped as Steinberger's wildly waving hand, secure in its super-grip glove, caught hold of a tree root protruding in a half-circle from the cliff face. His body tugged to an abrupt halt.

'Hold on, Steinberger,' Suave called, frantically trying to think how they could save him.

But Steinberger heard none of Suave's command as his eyes looked below him. His breath quickened as the reality of his situation spread like a slow stain into his mind. If he couldn't hold on, he was seconds away from a plunging drop that would deliver him into the gaping jaws of a devastating death.

CHAPTER 15

A TREACHEROUS RESCUE AND A PERILOUS PURSUIT

Max pulled her super-grip gloves on more tightly. She took a deep breath, trying to steady her nerves as she prepared to cross the ravine to save the dangling Steinberger.

'No. I've got a better plan.' It was Suave.

'But he needs our help,' Linden objected.

Suave never wanted Steinberger on this mission, Max thought suspiciously. Now he's going to let him die! 'I'm not going to stand here and do nothing while . . .' she began, but Suave wasn't listening.

'Steinberger!' he called across the ravine. 'Breathe deeply and slowly. Your gloves will keep you attached, but it is up to you to pull yourself to the top.'

Steinberger did nothing as a gust of wind bullied him with a sharp shove into the cliff.

'I believe you can do this,' Suave called again.

Still nothing.

'You have come so far and faced other fears head-on. Now you need to do that again.'

Steinberger's breath squeezed out of his lungs in reluctant bursts.

'We have to go and help him,' Max demanded.

'Steinberger.' Suave tried another tack. 'Frond needs you.'

Steinberger looked up.

'She's counting on us,' Suave continued. 'Breathe calmly.'

The mention of Frond filled Steinberger's arms with renewed strength. The thought of her needing their help steadied his panicked thoughts.

'You have your harness on so all you need to do now is throw the attached Abseiler. Aim it at the boulder on the cliff above you. Retract the rope and use it to winch yourself to safety.'

It was a good plan, Max conceded, one she hoped Steinberger's nerves and arms were up to.

'Come on, Steinberger,' Linden whispered.

With slow, steady movements, Steinberger did as he was told and, as he imagined Frond standing at the top of his cliff, just out of his sight, the Abseiler pulled him to safety.

When he reached the top, he somehow seemed taller, more composed than Max had seen him since they'd crashlanded. Within minutes he had his Abseiler in hand and threw it to the other side of the cliff, where it made a secure landing on the tree beside Max. 'Go, Steinberger.' Max was impressed and watched every move as the agent made his calm and agile way towards them.

Max and Linden grabbed his hands as he grabbed at the cliff in front of them.

'Well done, Steinberger. I knew you could do it,' Suave beamed.

'Yeah. Some of the finest work I've seen from you,' Linden nodded.

Steinberger shrugged his shoulders and looked directly at Suave. 'Thank you.'

'My pleasure.' Suave blushed. 'OK, everyone. Let's pack up and keep moving.'

Max watched as Suave and Steinberger consulted the map to make sure they were on course. Even after a plane crash and a daring climb across a ravine, Suave looked calm. Maybe he was good after all. He really had saved Steinberger's life when he could have let him fall, but she still couldn't ignore the stare he had given her at Spy Force or the guilty look he had worn after the muffin fell out of his bag.

Linden moved beside her as she finished packing away her Abseiler. 'I thought we'd lose Steinberger for a minute there.'

'Yeah, until action boy stepped in to play superhero.' Max leant against a bulge in a tree next to her.

It was obvious by Linden's frown what he was thinking.

'I know I'm being unfair, but I'm just having an unreasonable moment, OK?'

'Sure,' Linden smiled. 'I'll be here when you're done.' He stared at her as if waiting for her to say more.

Max tried to stay quiet, knowing what she had to say would come out all wrong, but the way Linden was looking at her made her want to blurt it out.

'It's just that he's so perfect all the time! How does he do it? He's always polite, calm, he never loses his temper and he's always in control. I mean, look at him. After all we've been through, there isn't a scratch or a scrap of dust on him.'

'Yeah, it's a pain having someone so good on a mission with us.' Linden raised his eyebrows sarcastically.

Max sighed. 'That's just it. I would have gone back for Steinberger but his plan was more clever and less risky.'

'Max, you're a great spy. Suave being so good doesn't change that.'

Max's shoulders sank. 'It'd help if he messed up. Even if it was only once.'

Linden laughed as a sharp screech of monkeys whooped above their heads, sending the upper branches of the trees above into a frenzied sway.

'This place is creepy.' Max looked around. 'I feel like I'm in the middle of *The Jungle Book*. And what's that smell?'

All around them were towering ancient trees strung with vines or bulging with lumpy outgrowths speckled with green algae.

'This tree even feels a bit like fur.'

'Ah, Max?' Linden eyed the brown mass she was leaning against. 'I think it is fur.'

'Fur? On a tree?'

Just then, two giant eyes opened next to Max's head. She stared as what she had thought was bark started up a slow, deep growl.

'I think it's a sloth, and I'm not sure he was ready to be woken up.' Linden couldn't help but smile as Max sprang away from the huge beast. She tripped over a clump of swollen roots and landed face first on the forest floor.

Linden stared at the animal in fascination. 'Isn't it beautiful?'

'Are we talking about the same animal?' Max looked at the ground beneath her, which was a thick, mossy, mud-covered mess.

'Sloths spend most of their lives hanging upside down.'

'Sounds fascinating.' Max gingerly peeled

herself from her muddied resting place just as she heard Suave and Steinberger approach behind her.

'According to what we've pieced together from Frond's second message and the detailed maps on our palm computers,' Suave announced importantly, 'there should be a track north of here that will lead us to her.'

Great, Max thought as she wiped forest muck from her shirt, now Suave's going to think he's on a mission with the world's greatest ignoramus. She turned round slowly to face them, ready for their look of horror.

Max's trousers were torn, her hair was matted with dirt and sweat, and her shoes were scuffed and soaked with mud. Suave, on the other hand, hadn't even broken out in a sweat. It was obvious how ridiculous Max looked, but he didn't seem to notice.

'So, let's get on with our mission.'

Suave turned and entered the jungle. Great branches crisscrossed before them, and each step on the damp rainforest floor was an exercise in ducking, weaving, and climbing over fallen trees the size of small cars. Max desperately tried to keep up with Suave, who manoeuvred through the jungle as if it was a stroll through a park.

Finally they came across the track they were

looking for. Suave double-checked the instructions and announced emphatically, 'This is it.' He looked to his right. 'And we're headed this way.'

Max and Linden reached for their water bottles. The heat had sucked the moisture from their throats and soaked them in their own pools of sweat.

'There isn't a sunnier route?' Max looked down the track which was a cavernous enclosure. It was covered by thick, gnarled branches that twisted overhead, cutting a dark trail beneath the blocked-out sun. The rich greens of the jungle disappeared as the darkness sucked the colour from everything, leaving a stained and blackened shadow. The ground was damp and the heat and fresh breeze was replaced by the smell of decay clogging the air. As they entered the enclosure the noise of the jungle died away and they were surrounded by an eerie quiet.

Max and Linden had a bad feeling about their new route.

'Onwards we go!' Suave's enthusiasm was like a runaway train.

Before anyone could move, they heard a low menacing rumble behind them that seemed to be coming from deep within the sheltered path.

‘I know the wildlife here is unique, but that doesn’t sound like any animal I know.’ Linden looked around him, trying to spot the source of the noise.

Then he saw it.

Through the thick tree trunks, they could see two beams of light winding their way towards them. The way they were approaching, it was obvious someone was in a hurry.

‘What makes me think they’re not the welcoming committee?’ Linden gulped.

Suave took a small rubber cube from his pocket and, giving his hand a shake, threw it into the air, where it unfolded before them into the Aqua Buggy.

‘Now might be a good time to pick up the pace. Hop in.’

Suave jumped into the driver’s seat as the others sprang in quickly behind him. He turned on the lights and a flurry of bats swarmed towards them in a terrified shriek. Max, Linden, and Steinberger’s hands instinctively flew to their heads as Suave checked the buggy’s controls, oblivious of the shrieking animals.

‘Buckle up, everyone!’

He then started the engine and took off at full speed.

Max gripped her armrest as she was flung around in the back seat, feeling as if she'd fallen into a washing machine. Great walls of solid bark were only narrowly avoided as Suave swept the steering wheel one way then the other, as if he was a rally car driver desperate to take first place.

'Hang on!' Suave yelled over his shoulder as he prepared to drive over a huge tree root snaking across the ground.

Until he realized the snaking tree root *was* actually a snake.

'Anaconda!'

'Oh dear.' Steinberger closed his eyes, clutched on to his door even harder and moved his lips as if he was praying.

The Aqua Buggy swerved along the kinked and buckled track towards the snake. Max held on and imagined the ill-placed reptile splattered in a sprawl of snake mush.

But Suave had other ideas.

He reached beside him and pressed a small red button marked *Airborne*. Within half a micro second, the Aqua Buggy was sailing over the snake, landing on the other side in a bumpy but expert manoeuvre. Max was pleased the snake was still alive, but her stomach was starting to have a few problems with the constant jolts, twists, and turns.

She turned back to see the anaconda slide into the forest just as a vehicle behind them skidded into view, flinging a wall of mud into the air.

'They're gaining on us!'

'Oh, dear.' Steinberger swallowed hard, trying not to throw up.

In the rear-view mirror, Max saw Suave's wide grin, before he pressed down even harder on the accelerator. She turned round, and it was then she noticed something. There were two men in the car, but the one behind the wheel reminded her of someone she knew. She couldn't place the heavy features or the look of pure malice on his face, but when his eyes locked on to hers, a cold shiver of fear formed in her veins.

Linden called out over the noise of the engine. 'Something tells me this guy isn't happy to see us.'

'I think I know him,' Max yelled back.

'You know someone here in the Amazon?'

'I know it sounds weird but it's true.'

Before her mind had a chance to figure out who he was, the Aqua Buggy came to an abrupt stop.

'Why have we stopped?'

There was no need to answer as she saw that

the road had ended at the edge of a fast-moving river that was so wide Max couldn't see the other side.

'The Amazon River,' Suave announced, as if he'd just discovered El Dorado, the fabled city of gold.

Max turned again as the vehicle behind them skidded to a stop. The man with the malicious grin stepped out and eyed them like a lion approaching an injured gazelle. He was a tall hulk of a man, with thick features and limbs like miniature tree trunks.

He lumbered a few steps towards them before pulling out a phone, his face dripping with victory.

Suave stared at the river as a giant tree trunk swept by. The Aqua Buggy was strong, but so was the current.

Steinberger read his thoughts. 'Will the Buggy cope?'

'I'm sure of it,' he answered confidently, reaching for the keys in the ignition. 'Hold on, everyone.'

The engine whined as it struggled to start.

'This isn't a great time for engine trouble,' Linden said, shaking his head.

Max watched as the two men lifted stun blasters as they walked towards the buggy. That's when Max remembered who he was. 'It's Kronch!' she told Linden. Kronch was Blue's assistant from their second mission. The same sausage fingers, the same overstuffed arms, the same neanderthal plod and lack of neck. With his monkey-brained partner, Kronch slowly made his way towards them. A snivelling grin wiped across his face as he aimed his blaster straight at Max.

Suave tried again and again to start the vehicle, but it choked and spluttered and refused to start.

Max stared at the churning waters of the Amazon River as Kronch broke into a wheezing laugh behind them. They were cornered like caged rats and it seemed there was nothing they could do to avoid capture.

CHAPTER 16

PLAN B AND AN UNEXPECTED FALL

Max, Linden, Suave, and Steinberger sat strapped into the Aqua Buggy as Kronch and his bumbling partner approached like overfed elephants, enjoying every second of their captives' nervous anticipation of doom.

Suave went straight into his usual man-of-action routine. 'OK, team, it's time for Plan B.'

Plan B? Why did he sound as if he was the overpaid lead in some corny, B-grade film? The one where the hero always has perfect hair and knows what to do. Max looked at him. Suave still had perfect hair. Even after all they'd been through.

'What's Plan B?' Linden asked, eager to avoid the sausage hands of Kronch.

Suave undid his seatbelt and pulled his laser from his pocket. 'Jump in here, and when I tell you, turn the key.'

Linden undid his belt and scrambled into the driver's seat. In seconds, Suave had the bonnet open. Sparks flew from either side of the buggy as he worked to fix the stalled engine. 'Start her up!'

'He's a mechanic too?' Max asked incredulously. 'Where does it end?'

Linden turned the key. Again, the engine wheezed, turning in a broken rhythm, until finally it came to life.

'Excellent,' Steinberger breathed.

Suave slammed the bonnet shut and resumed his place as driver.

Kronch and his sidekick exchanged an amused look. With the river on one side and their truck blocking the path, where could their captives go?

'So long, boys!' Max called, as Suave shifted the engine into first gear and drove off the bank and straight into the river.

Before the buggy was submerged Max caught the look of confusion on Kronch's face and savoured every dazed second of it.

'It's really going to strain Kronch's brain trying to figure out what just happened.' Linden smiled at Max as the Aqua Buggy submarined through the waters of the river.

'It'll do his brain good to get some exercise,' Max joked, before turning to Steinberger. 'That was Kronch. He was . . .' she began to explain, until she saw the look of terror suctioned on to his face. 'Steinberger?'

He didn't answer.

Every second of this mission took him into a new territory of fear, but there hadn't been one moment where he had complained or even hinted at backing out. He may have looked awkward with his thin body, long limbs, and desperate fear of bugs, but when it came to being brave, Steinberger was the most courageous of all of them.

He stared rigidly at the water-filled windows around them. The view was filled with fish, eels, and giant tangled walls of reeds swaying sharply in the forceful current. Max guessed Steinberger had never even been swimming in his life, going by his look of gasping suffocation. Sweat was running freely down his forehead and soaking into his already damp and bedraggled suit. His breath heaved in and out in quick, sharp jabs. He hadn't heard a word Max had said. She tried again gently.

'Steinberger?'

He jumped. 'Yes?'

'Linden and I recognized the man in the car behind us.'

'You did?' He calmed a little.

'It was Kronch. One of Blue's thugs from Mission Blue's Foods.* It must mean Blue is involved and knows we're here.'

'*The* Mr Blue?' Suave said with a streak of excitement in his voice.

'That's not a good thing,' Max clarified.

* See *Max Remy Spy Force: Spy Force Revealed*

'No, of course not.'

'What do we do now, Steinberger?' After nearly losing his life the last time they met Blue, Linden wasn't keen to bump into him again.*

Just then the Buggy tilted sharply to one side as Suave turned to avoid a giant electric eel.

'Oh dear!' Steinberger was having trouble breathing again.

'We're getting close to finding Frond. Right?' Max prompted, eager to stop Steinberger freaking out.

As if that name had some kind of tonic in it, Steinberger's demeanour instantly changed. He sat upright, threw his chest out, and took a deep breath.

'You're right. We have a mission to complete and lives to save.'

Steinberger took out his palm computer and began checking the coordinates of where they were and how to get back on track to find Frond. He leant forward and gave the directions to Suave.

Max sighed, then caught sight of a crooked smile on Linden's face.

'What?'

* See *Max Remy Spy Force: The Hollywood Mission*

'Sometimes, Max Remy, you can be the nicest person I know,' he whispered.

She instantly blushed. 'Don't get too used to it.'

Despite the warning, Linden's smile became even bigger. Max tried to resist it but it was no good and she had to give in to her own wide grin.

As Steinberger finished his directions, Suave gripped the steering wheel in excitement. 'OK, everyone, Plan B is over. It's time for Plan C.'

'This better be good,' Max groaned. With the ride through the forest and the force of the current nudging them from side to side, her stomach was ready for a steadier ride. But when Suave pressed harder on the accelerator and pulled the steering wheel towards him, the Aqua Buggy's nose rose up like a plane during take-off.

'Oh dear,' Max and Steinberger said in unison.

Within seconds, the Buggy broke through the surface of the river and bobbed on its rippling surface. Its wheels started turning, moving it forward like an inflatable paddleboat.

'Woo hoo!' Suave whooped as he wound down his window. 'This is beautiful!'

The others wound down their windows as the cloudless blue sky and a flood of sun spread around them. Great mountains of trees clung to the rich brown banks that acted as muddy slides for alligators and turtles. Birds of all sizes and colours swooped in and out of branches and dived for fish just below the river's surface.

'The Amazon is the second-longest river in the world after the Nile in Africa,' explained Suave. 'It's so big in parts, many people refer to it as the Ocean River.'

Max turned away from Suave's nature documentary voice-over to see small islands peppered across the river's surface.

'Not the kind of place you want to dangle your feet, though,' Linden advised.

'What do you mean?'

'Look.' Linden pointed to an island they were sailing past just in time for Max to see the sharpened teeth and scaly body of an alligator leap out of the water and seize an unsuspecting turtle in its flattened snout.

'I see what you mean,' said Max, winding her window up a little.

The Aqua Buggy manoeuvred through the churning waters of the Amazon River like a miniature ferry. Steinberger held on tight, trying not to concentrate on the rise and fall of chocolatey waves. The water lapped against the side of the vehicle, turning and swirling as they were lifted up and down on its deep swell. Max noticed Steinberger's eyelids becoming heavy, his head leaning out of his window, as if struggling to stay upright.

'Steinberger, are you OK?'

He didn't answer. Max turned to Linden. 'He must have the sleeping sickness!'

Suave turned from the driver's seat and studied his complexion. 'I think it's seasickness,' he said with a knowing nod.

Max panicked. 'Well, maybe you're wrong.' Her eyes narrowed, challenging Suave, but just as she was about to say more, Steinberger vomited out of the window of the Buggy.

'Or maybe it is seasickness,' Linden suggested, holding on to Steinberger's jacket to stop him from toppling overboard.

'Sorry about that.' Steinberger sat back in his seat, embarrassed about what had just happened. 'I've never had very good sea legs. Even on a river, so it seems.'

'That's OK.' Max patted Steinberger's hand, but was distracted by the view outside the window. The current of the river seemed to be getting stronger.

The message light on Steinberger's computer flashed.

'Is it Frond?' Linden asked.

Steinberger opened the message. 'No. It's from Alex. She sent it a few minutes ago.'

'Steinberger, it's Alex,' a sombre recording announced. 'I'm afraid the situation here has become very serious. Agent Steeple has fallen into a coma. Her vital signs are extremely weak and Finch has placed her in a humidicrib with an intravenous drip filled with extra-potent vitamins to keep her alive. Time is very much against us.'

Steinberger took a deep breath in an effort to drive away the final twinges of seasickness, and sent a message back. 'Dear Alex, do not worry. Mission Triatoma is proceeding well. Ensure the Goliath is at the Invisible Jet in the next few hours.' He thought again, before adding, 'The fate of Steeple and all the agents of Spy Force is in good hands.'

Max looked at his screen as he sent the message. 'It is, isn't it, Steinberger?'

Steinberger smiled. 'Couldn't be in better, Max.'

As he put the computer away, a quiet roaring sound swirled towards them from downriver.

'Can you hear that?' Max looked around, trying to see what it was.

'Oh good, you can hear it too.' Linden was relieved. 'I thought it might be my stomach even though it sounded like something a little bigger.'

'Something *much* bigger, if I'm not mistaken,' Suave said.

Max clenched her teeth. 'And what would that be?'

Suave listened for a few more seconds.

'A waterfall.'

Max looked in front of her. All she could see was river.

'A waterfall?'

'Yep, and from the height of that spray, I'd say it's a big one. Hold on, everyone, I'll try and take us to the bank.' Then he added, 'And you might want to wind up your windows.'

They did as he suggested while Suave grabbed the controls and did all he could to manoeuvre the Buggy out of the current's jostling, speeding grip.

Steinberger, Max, and Linden could now see it too. A haze of rising mist and a faraway boiling of water. 'How high do you think it is?' Steinberger asked gingerly.

'A few hundred metres,' Suave answered

calmly, as if he was talking about the height of something safe like a bridge or a building, and not a crushing torrent they couldn't possibly survive.

Max and Linden now clearly saw the edge of the waterfall frothing along the horizon. There was a frenzy of water leading to a white haze of nothingness. Like the end of the world, Max thought as they were sucked closer.

Suave's face held a small but determined smile as he worked at the controls of the Buggy.

'Is there a Plan D?' Linden asked hopefully.

'Not sure yet,' Suave answered as he desperately tried to move them out of the path of the waterfall, but it was no good. The force of the current held them firmly as it hauled them towards the waterfall's plunging, deadly edge.

CHAPTER 17

AN UNUSUAL CATCH AND A TERRIBLE DISCOVERY

'Linden, there's something I have to tell you!' Max shouted over the noise of the crashing wall of water, as the waterfall rained over them.

'What?' Linden struggled to hear Max, whose words were consumed by the churning waves boiling around them.

The Aqua Buggy shifted and rolled over the frenzied torrent. Steinberger clung on to his armrest as Suave continued to fight the increasingly futile battle to save their lives.

'There's something I have to tell you!' Max and Linden had once before faced possible death by waterfall when they were taken to Mr Blue's mansion. Then, as now, she panicked and thought it was time to tell Linden how she felt about him. How he was the most important person in her life. How he was special. How without him life would be . . . how was she going to say it?

'It's just that I . . .'

She was interrupted by Suave calling out from the front. 'Be ready to evacuate when I give the word.'

And with that, Suave opened the sunroof, letting a torrent of water splash on Max like a bucket of water. He clung to the sides of the sunroof and hoisted himself out of the Buggy and onto the roof.

'Evacuate where?' Max yelled up through the wash, annoyed at how much Suave seemed to be enjoying their impending doom.

Just then, they felt a heavy jolt on the roof.

'That's a *good* jolt, right?' Linden winced.

Above the thunderous pounding of water, they heard the sound of an engine coming to life, and great whopping blades slowly turning above them.

'The Heliocraft!' Linden cried. He wound down his window and looked to see the flying inflatable vehicle gleaming in the brilliant sun, ready for take-off. Suave beamed through the clear cabin and gave him the thumbs-up.

'Looks like we're going flying, agents.'

Max looked at the waterfall, then at the spinning blades above them, and knew she had little choice. Linden helped her climb out of the window into a swirling mass of wind and water, and, gripping the Heliocraft's sturdy skids, she pulled herself into the craft.

'Your turn, Steinberger.' Linden tried to look as unfazed as he could, while every passing moment brought the waterfall even closer.

'O-OK,' Steinberger stammered.

The river tossed the buggy like a ship in a storm, but with Linden behind him and Max leaning out of the craft above him, there were only a few near falls before the soaking Administration Manager was nestled into the Heliocraft and buckled into his seat.

Moments later, a dripping Linden climbed in beside them and gave the biggest ever grin to Suave.

'Ready for take-off, captain.' Linden was enjoying every second of their escape.

The Heliocraft's skids lifted into the air just in time to see the Aqua Buggy torpedo over the edge of the waterfall and disappear in a crushing, white oblivion.

'Quimby's not going to be happy when we tell her about that.' Linden shook his head and released a shower of water over everyone. There was a moment of silence from the agents as they took in what had just happened.

Especially the fact that they were still alive.

'Woo hoo! Are we good or what?' Steinberger whooped and punched the air.

Max and Linden giggled.

'I mean . . . that's good . . . what just happened.'

Then they heard a weird water-clogged hum, as if a swarm of boulder-sized bees had pulled up beside them, but before Max could think about it any further, a large chopper appeared above them. Two spinning circular saws hung from its underside.

'That can't be good.' Linden watched as the spinning discs aimed straight for the Heliocraft's blades.

Suave tried to fly lower but he was too late. The high-pitched whine of metal on metal wrenched the air.

The Heliocraft plunged a few metres before being wrenched to an abrupt stop by a net and swinging into a pendulum-style swoop.

'Where are we going?' Max clung to her seatbelt and guessed wherever it was, it wouldn't be fun.

'Not sure,' Suave answered, as if he was on a joy flight. 'But that's the FZ-511. One of the finest choppers you'll find.'

'You mean the chopper that's holding us prisoner and destroyed Quimby's Heliocraft?' Max looked at him sternly.

'Yeah.'

'Maybe this is what happens when you die?' Linden was feeling surprisingly calm.

Max frowned. 'A giant helicopter appears from the sky and carries us in a net to some kind of happy ever after?'

Linden winced. 'I knew it'd sound silly if I said it out loud.'

The chopper thundered above as it carried them over the exploding plume of green jungle until it came to a gap in the trees. It then dropped the mutilated Heliocraft with a rude jolt before rising from the clearing and flying away.

The four agents climbed out. Before them stood a sprawling two-storey mansion, settled deep within the jungle. It was painted stark white and was somehow out of place but curiously at home as well. Deep green vines crept up the two columns that proudly guarded the entrance. A set of marble stairs poured into a pebbled drive and led to a gently bubbling fountain. Shutters shielded each window and a broad veranda swooped around the lower floor, filled with chairs and tables like a hotel awaiting the arrival of a tour bus. The whole scene was surrounded by a perfectly manicured lawn jutting up against the tangled jungle.

'Where are we?' Max asked.

'Not sure, but I don't think solid ground ever felt this good,' Linden said, taking a deep breath.

'I agree with you there.' Steinberger offered him a weak smile. He surveyed the surroundings and noticed a series of signal towers and satellite dishes positioned on the mansion's roof.

'Wherever we are, it is certainly well connected. Judging by their size, those towers and dishes are capable of picking up an incredible range of signals from great distances, and are equipped with a communication barrier to stop unwanted messages getting in and out or being detected by unwanted elements. I know because we had our communications systems updated to a similar set-up only six months ago.'

There was one device on the roof Steinberger wasn't sure about. A large cannon-like object pointed towards the sky. Something bothered him about it, but he wasn't sure what.

Linden stared at the roof. 'Which means they could have been the reason Frond's message was corrupted.'

'Very clever, Linden.' Suave flashed a toothpaste smile.

'So she's here?' Max asked.

'Let's hope so.' Steinberger checked his computer and smiled broadly. 'This is the place her directions lead to.'

A low growl and stirring of trees was heard nearby.

'You all heard that, right?' Linden asked.

'Yep. My guess is it's dogs.' Suave sniffed the air. He crouched to the ground and placed both hands on the soil. 'Roger that. Dogs.'

Three snarling dogs pushed their way through the dense undergrowth and slowly crept towards them. Their growling bit into Max's nerves like giant mosquitoes.

Ones that could kill you.

'Is it just me or does it seem like these dogs haven't been fed for a while?' Linden looked at their salivating jaws and edgy pacing.

'If we don't make any sudden moves we should be all right.' Suave stared at the approaching animals.

That was it. Max had had all she could take of Mr Encyclopaedia—the calmness, the always knowing what to do, the never being scared. She spun round and threw her hands firmly onto her hips.

'Are you going to keep being so perfect? This whole mission you have done nothing but do everything right and you haven't even the slightest idea of how annoying that is.'

Max took in deep breaths, knowing that Suave being so clever wasn't the best excuse she had for yelling at him.

Suave looked confused. 'Sorry, Max.'

'And stop apologizing. That's annoying too.'

'Ah, Max?' It was Linden. 'I don't think the dogs like you getting so upset.'

Max felt hot panting against her neck. She turned slowly to see the long dripping fangs of one of the dogs. 'Right. I'll be still from now on.'

A shrill whistle pierced the air and the dogs turned from salivating killers into puppies leaping and galloping towards the mansion steps. The click of stun blasters sounded behind the agents' heads.

'Won't you come in?'

Max immediately knew it was Kronch's beefy voice behind them. She also knew they had no choice but to do as he said.

They were marched across the pebbled driveway, up the marble steps, and into a pristine foyer, with light filtering through the many windows in speckled waves. Chandeliers hung like clumps of diamonds from tall ceilings and the walls were covered in grand paintings that stood above carved stands with ornate vases. It was hard to reconcile this peaceful European-style palace with the sweltering heat and animal-filled jungle outside.

They stood in their wet, crumpled clothes as a

cool air-conditioned breeze wafted over them, sighing in relief as if they'd been plunged into a deep crystal-blue pool. Their relief, however, was cut short by a voice from the top of the stairs.

'I decided we'd had enough fun toying with you and it was time to invite you in.'

'Blue! I knew you were behind this,' Suave announced.

Really, Sherlock? Max grumbled silently before turning to Blue. 'If this is an *invitation*, I'm busy and have to get going.' She threw out her chin until she felt the point of the stun blaster in her back.

'Maybe we could stay for a bit?' Linden suggested. Letting Blue have his way for now would give them time to think of a plan.

'Excellent. I have so many things to show you I think you'll find interesting.'

Blue had this creepy habit of finding out secret information few people knew and Max had a feeling he had done it again and had every intention of using it against them.

'Besides, Steinberger and I are old friends. It wouldn't be right for us not to have a chance to catch up. Talk about old times.'

Max saw Steinberger's face harden. She knew Blue held Steinberger partly responsible for his dismissal from Spy Force. Maybe he'd even use this chance to get his revenge.

'Where's Frond?'

'Who?' Blue spoke with an irritating innocence.

'Frond. Where is she?' Steinberger tensed up, his voice cold and hard.

'It's been a long time since I was on the Force,' Blue pronounced pointedly. 'If you've misplaced one of your agents, that's hardly my problem.'

Steinberger knew he was lying and moved forward to make him tell the truth, but was held back just in time by Linden. 'He's only trying to upset you.'

Steinberger calmed down. He would find Frond with or without Blue's assistance. For now, though, they'd have to play along with his games.

'Drinks, anyone?' Blue clapped his hands and a white-suited waiter pushed through a swinging door holding trays of tropical drinks.

'No thanks. I think I'll pass on being poisoned for today.' Max was trying to stay calm but there was something about Blue that always made her furious.

The swirling heat of the jungle had dropped to a bearable level in Blue's mansion but those drinks sat before them like little islands of gold. Knowing how much they would have loved one, Blue reached for a glass and slowly sipped every last refreshing drop of a sweet, cold mango juice.

'Perfect.' Blue ushered the drinks away and Linden only just held back from running after them. 'Since you're in such a hurry, we'd better get on with the tour of my new enterprise.'

With Kronch and his meat-headed friend behind them, the four agents followed Blue up the winding staircase. Max ran her hand along the banisters, which were carved into creeping vines and led them to a large ornately decorated corridor lined with framed paintings of crops and plantations.

'We mainly grow coffee, cocoa, and soya beans. We also have cotton, rice, cassava, and mangoes, as well as a very healthy rubber plantation.'

'So you've traded evil for the life of a farmer?'

Blue turned his head slowly. 'Oh, Maxine, I do miss your fiery little ways when we're apart.'

Max tensed. 'It's Max,' she said through clenched teeth.

Linden knew Max hated being talked down to and gently squeezed her hand to calm her down. He also knew what Max was getting at. Blue was much too cunning to simply be planting crops.

Blue opened a large wooden door that led to a dark room. Floral wallpaper lined three walls, while the fourth was covered by a long curtain of deep red. Small tables holding bowls of fruit and chocolates sat between giant leather sofas. In one corner was a control panel filled with knobs, lights, and buttons, and above this were positioned several security cameras showing views all around Blue's property.

'Please, come in. Make yourself comfortable.'

Max would never get used to his creepy smile or the lilting tone of his voice that dripped with pure malice. Being comfortable in Blue's presence was something even his own mother must have found hard to do.

Blue strode to a throne-like chair with painted gold borders and floral embroidered cushions. Behind him was a life-sized portrait of himself, sitting in an eerily similar position.

Max, Steinberger, Linden, and Suave sat on two sofas opposite, with Kronch and his friend standing guard at the door.

'During my time at Spy Force,' Blue said, 'I happened to find out that Harrison Senior was experimenting with the creation of an elixir of life that could allow a person to live for hundreds of years. The experiment was, of course, very hush

hush, but as soon as he'd finished his elixir, he realized it was one of the greatest moments in the history of science. Harrison Senior also knew that it could lead to untold problems, such as overpopulation in an already crowded world, so he destroyed it, but not before recording the recipe in a top secret location.'

Blue selected a chocolate from the bowl beside him and took his time with every savoured chew. 'They taste so much better when they are made from fresh cocoa beans.'

Suave was losing patience with Blue's speech. 'What does any of this have to do with us?'

Blue licked his lips. 'You're just about to find out. You see, I also know that Harrison's father had an assistant in his experiment.'

Blue pressed a button on his armchair and the curtain slid aside. Below them a vast laboratory was operating behind the thick shield of glass. Steinberger, Max, Linden, and Suave stood up to get a better look. There were lab-coated technicians moving amongst boiling glass cylinders, inspecting rows of test tubes filled with multi-coloured substances and stirring giant vats and barrels bubbling with steaming concoctions.

'This is my distillery. You see, the people of the

Amazon have been creating natural cures for their ills for hundreds of years and we plan to take that knowledge to the world. Essentially we take plant and animal matter from the jungle and extract powerful cures and potions. From plants, bark, fish eggs . . . even bugs.'

Max and Linden gave each other a quick look.

'And you thought you'd just waltz in and take the knowledge of centuries for yourself.' Max was indignant. It was obvious Blue's tour was to prove to them that he was the one who had placed the sleeping sickness in Spy Force.

'Maxine.' Blue smiled sweetly as he moved beside them. 'I'm not going to rise to your chiding. I've been on quite a successful anger management course and even you will not be able to rile me. And I must admit that being among the simple purity and serenity of nature has made me a different man. More harmonious, more in tune with life, more . . .'

'Full of it?' Max scoffed.

Linden smirked but immediately remembered where they were. He wasn't sure he wanted to test the limits of Blue's new-found serenity.

'Ah, there she is. The most important item I wanted to show you.'

The agents looked down into the lab. Kronch and his bulbous partner giggled at the alarm pasted to their faces.

It was Frond.

Dressed in her bright red coat, with her distinctive beehive hairdo.

'Frond!' But it was no good. Max couldn't be heard behind the thick glass. Frond busily moved about Blue's lab as easily as if she was at home in her Plantorium.

Steinberger pressed his hand on to the glass and stared down at the Spy Force agent seemingly working for the enemy.

'With her knowledge of plants, she is my perfect companion in the Amazon. So many rare and as yet unknown species to work with. It's been said that the people of the forest know cures for diseases we never thought possible. I knew with such a vast and unlimited array of plants to work with, Frond would be only too happy to come and work with me.' At this he stood directly beside Steinberger. 'And we did get along famously when I was at Spy Force.'

Max saw Steinberger's cheeks tense as he clenched his teeth.

'She's a loyal little thing . . .' Blue paused

for effect, 'when it comes to her work.' He threw it out as a challenge, daring Steinberger to contradict him.

'Frond would never agree to work with you!' Max shouted.

Blue eyed her with pure enjoyment. 'Thing is, Maxine, she already has.'

Something about this last sentence sent tremors through all four agents. Max knew what she was seeing, but she also knew Frond would never choose to work with Blue.

'Can you see anything else of interest?' Blue said casually.

The agents scanned the area, until Linden saw something that made his heart jolt.

'The Spy Force manual,' he breathed. Frond was carefully turning its well-thumbed pages under a small lamp with a pink light bulb—the device needed for reading its secret experiments written in invisible ink.

'Yes!' Blue pronounced excitedly.

'But how . . .' Linden stared at the book that was the key to Spy Force.

Steinberger's fingers slowly flexed before curling into two rigid fists.

Max knew Blue was toying with them like a

bully about to pull the wings off a fly.

'Oh, that part is such fun—and it was only possible with the help of a few of the wonderful agents of Spy Force itself.'

Max shot Suave a hard look. Maybe it was now that she would discover he was the crooked agent.

'You see, many years ago I accidentally walked in on Frond, Harrison, and his father recording something in the back of the Spy Force manual, and I knew by the way they guarded it so secretively that it was something very important and that, therefore, I had to have it. But before I could investigate further, I was rudely expelled from the Force.' He turned to Steinberger. 'I won't go into those details now, as Steinberger knows that story only too well, seeing as he was a central part of the whole dirty business.'

Steinberger eyed Blue carefully. He wasn't going to bite at his flawed retelling of history.

'For years I've been trying to infiltrate Spy Force, but with CRISP doing such a fine job keeping it impenetrable, I thought if I can't get in, I'll get someone inside to do my work for me.'

'So the stolen manual was an inside job, just like Dretch said,' Linden deduced.

'Ah, Dretch,' Blue smiled. 'He was simply

excellent. He slipped in that poisoned food sample and didn't flinch once when he retrieved the manual. He really is one top notch but neglected agent.'

'Dretch is one of Spy Force's most loyal agents and would never do what you're suggesting.' Steinberger was standing firm.

'Loyalty is no match when it comes to my new invention.' Blue sniggered quietly.

Max and Linden shifted nervously.

'My Mind Control Frequency Satellite.'

The declaration hung in the air like just delivered bad news.

'And Frond is . . .' Steinberger looked forlornly at his beloved Frond, a stab of jealousy eating into him, as he now realized she too was under Blue's control.

'Yes.' Blue's eyes flared. 'Her too.'

'How is it possible?' Suave asked, not sure what to believe.

'It emits a high frequency signal that invades a person's thinking and alters it to do exactly as I dictate and all I needed to achieve this brain break-in was a DNA sample from my lucky chosen few. With Dretch, I still had a postcard he'd sent me from a holiday he once took in

Sweden. His DNA was perfectly preserved on the stamp.'

'And Frond?' Linden asked warily.

'Well, you see, I had a very special fondness for Frond when I was at the Force, even though the feeling never seemed to have been reciprocated.'

'It's because she has something called taste,' Max spelt out.

Blue ignored Max's comments and went on. 'One day I came across her handbag and inside was a comb with one of her beautiful strands of hair. I took the hair and have kept it in my wallet ever since. Clever, if you really think about it.'

'Creepy is what I'd call it.' Max shivered at the new level of weird Blue had just reached.

'So I had Dretch steal the manual and leave it in the Plantorium. Once I'd begun the mind control on Frond, she took the precious book, wrote her farewell note and brought it directly to me. No fuss, no bother, and no messy kidnap scenes. They can be such a bore. And now I really have been talking too long. I must get back to my new recruit and see how her work is coming along.'

Blue could hardly contain his joy at having Spy Force's Administration Manager in his hands. If this was his way of getting revenge, by the hurt look on Steinberger's face, it seemed he'd succeeded.

'Take them away.'

Blue's two thugs latched themselves on to the agents, like guard dogs waiting for the command from their master.

'And relieve them of their packs. They won't be needing those where they're going.'

'Whatever you have in mind, Blue, nothing will stand in the way of us accomplishing our mission.' Suave struggled in the thick arms of his captor.

'Go get 'em, cowboy,' Max mumbled to herself, but it was exactly what she'd wanted to say as they were pinioned by the goons and led away from Frond and into the clutches of Blue's latest loathsome plan.

CHAPTER 18

A CAN OF WORMS AND AN IMPORTANT DEDUCTION

'You know you'll never beat us,' Suave declared as they were led away from Blue. 'We're Spy Force agents and we always complete our mission.'

'Now he's sounding like a Canadian mountie,' Max sighed.

The four agents were led down a series of hidden passageways, through dusty and forgotten rooms and moist and clammy cellars. Max flung herself about wildly to be as annoying as she could but, catching Linden's eye, was reminded to keep her temper and not make the goons upset.

Kronch had removed their packs and thrown them into a rubbish bin just outside the kitchen. He then stayed at the rear, his stun blaster jamming into Steinberger's back every chance he got.

The other thug remained at the front. His hulking body swayed from side to side as he thumped his way through the passages to a set of muddy steps. He stopped before a splintered and roughly hewn door and, placing a large key into a rusting iron lock, led the agents to their final destination.

'Don't worry, agents, I have a plan,' Suave announced confidently.

The room was dark and moist. The ground was

spongy and slippery and smelt of damp earth and mouldy food.

'One of your best guest rooms, is it?' Max couldn't help it. She knew it was better to stay quiet but she couldn't let these goons get away without any attitude. Kronch and his partner didn't answer as they tied the agents to a wooden pole in the centre of the room.

'Are you going to leave us here until we sprout mushrooms?'

Kronch let loose a snort-ridden laugh.

Max was confused. Until she looked up.

Above them was a giant metal chute with a transparent cover, behind which were imprisoned thousands of heaving worms.

'Worms?' Max thought Blue could do better than that.

'Did someone say worms?' Suave didn't look up.

'Thousands of them,' Linden sighed as he too saw the mass of slippery creatures wriggle and slime above them. 'I never thought I'd end my life as compost.'

'Worms? Thousands of them? What are they doing here? And what do we have to do with them?' Suave was sounding increasingly agitated. His voice lost its controlled edge and his pitch got higher and higher.

Max ignored him. 'Compost. That's it, Linden. We're about to become part of the world's biggest worm farm,' she deduced.

'Small . . . slimy . . . thousands.' Suave was really starting to lose it.

Kronch and his friend left the room and closed the door with a hammering thud. They took turns to keep watch through a small observation window.

'Why worms?' It was Suave again. 'Do you really think they'll release them?'

'Yep. Things tend to get like this when I'm on a mission.' Max squelched in the spongy ground.

'We don't have much time,' Steinberger announced. 'We must work out—'

But Steinberger was interrupted by something strange.

'We've got to get out of here!' Suave yelled. He thrashed about in his roped position, trying to break free. 'We'll die! Smothered by thousands of moist, slimy, miniature feeders of death. Crawling over the dead and rotting, eating their way through the earth, ruling the very soil we walk on, making our last moments on earth a simple food fest!' He thrashed about some more, and finally, after all they'd been through, his hair became ruffled from its perfect, sculptured coiffure.

Max stared, sure she couldn't really be seeing what she was seeing.

'I don't want to die! I don't want to become worm food. Please . . . I don't want to die! Mummy! Mummy!'

And with that, Suave fainted.

'Suave?' Steinberger nudged the limp body of Suave next to him.

'At least that'll keep him quiet for a while,' Max murmured.

Just then the transparent cover of the worm chute started to slide open.

'This is going to be really messy.' Linden braced himself as the first worms fell on his head and quickly disappeared into his propeller-shaped hair. 'Uh-oh. They could be in there for days.'

'Oh dear,' Steinberger's fear of bugs found new life. 'Do you think any of our bug repellent survived the waterfall?'

'Doubt it.' Max blinked as a worm fell on her face and quickly slid off. When she opened her eyes she saw Steinberger once again trying to be brave. 'Are you going to be OK with them?'

'Yes,' Steinberger shuddered. 'Quite.'

'You know, Steinberger,' Max smiled. 'I think you've been great on this mission.'

A few worms slimed down Steinberger's blushing face. 'I guess you don't know what you can do until something you love is taken from you.'

'Something you love?' Linden spat a worm from his lips.

'Yep, you don't easily forget someone who has given your life meaning, who has lifted you from what you are to what you could become and shown you how wonderful the world really can be.'

Linden gave Max a wink. He was finally going to do it. After years of not admitting it to anybody, Steinberger was finally going to admit his feelings for Frond. 'That must feel pretty amazing.'

'Yes, well,' Steinberger blushed. 'Spy Force is an amazing place.'

'Spy Force?' Linden and Max spluttered.

'Spy Force is the only family I have. I was six, and an only child, when my parents and I were driving up a beautiful mountain path in New Zealand. About halfway up, a huge storm hit and swept the car off the road and into a ravine. I can still remember the green and white snow-covered trees flashing past as our car bumped and turned to the bottom. Then it stopped. I called to my parents but they didn't answer. I was there for three days before the storm passed and a driver found and rescued me.'

Max blew a worm from her nose and stretched a rope-bound finger towards Steinberger. 'We'll save Spy Force, Steinberger. I know we will.' A bunch of worms slopped onto his shoulder.

As Suave continued to slump beside them, passed out in worm fear, Max desperately tried to work out what was going on. Again and again she saw the image of Frond working in Blue's lab as if she belonged there. As if she was happy to be part of his team. It wasn't right.

'I guess you can't always believe what you see.'

'Yep.' Linden agreed as a swamp of sucking, writhing worms was starting to build around their feet. 'Frond working for Blue, Dretch's fingerprints on the cabinet,' and here he looked at Max, 'Suave being perfect.'

Max looked away. 'I guess even perfect people have a weak spot.' She felt bad about suspecting Suave was bad and for being angry with him when all he was trying to be was a good agent.

'What should we do now?' she asked, closing her lips just in time to avoid a mouthful of worms.

'Find and destroy the mind control satellite,

rescue Frond and the manual, and meet the Goliath to take us back to Spy Force.'

'Great,' sighed Max. 'Simple, but where would Blue keep the device?'

Steinberger's ponderous look brightened. 'There's a cannon-like device on the roof of this mansion that is pointed directly into the sky. I didn't know what it was earlier, but after all we've learnt, I'd say it's feeding directly off a satellite and using the installed DNA samples to track down a person's location before invading their minds and controlling their thoughts.'

'I think you might be on to something, Steinberger,' Linden said proudly as the pool of worms rose up his legs.

'But if Frond is under Blue's control, how could she have sent us details of where she was?'

'My guess is this.' Steinberger squinted, concentrating hard. 'Blue used the device to make Frond take the book and leave Spy Force. She was brought here and then Blue turned off the machine hoping Frond would want to work for him, that she would finally fall for his charms. He would be vain enough to think she would. That's when she sent us the messages. When she wouldn't co-operate Blue knew he had no choice but to use the device again.'

'But how did she get through the Spy Force lock-down?' Max shrugged a worm out of her ear.

'Frond was in charge of the lock-down for the Plantorium. With the mind control, she would simply have walked through.'

'How are we going to get out of here?' Some worms had crawled inside Linden's shirt and were starting to tickle.

'Like this.' Steinberger wriggled his hand into his pocket and slowly took out his Hypnotron. 'I'm not good with packs—I have a tendency to lose them. So I put a few of Quimby's smaller gadgets in my pockets.'

He programmed a time limit. 'An hour should do it. It's time to complete Mission Triatoma.'

Kronch and the other goon had their backs to the observation window. 'We need to get their attention.'

'Max? I think this calls for your expertise.' Linden smiled mischievously. 'Brace yourself, Steinberger.'

Max took a deep breath and let out a huge scream. One of those girly screams that should come with a health warning for your ears. She did her best act of flinging herself about and being petrified of worms as the goons looked in and smiled, enjoying every minute.

'You won't think this is so funny.' Steinberger pointed the Hypnotron at the goons and an intense golden beam was directed into their eyes. After thirty seconds it stopped. 'That should do it. Come in,' he called.

The goons obediently opened the door and waded through the squelching waist-high worm goo towards them.

'Cut the ropes.'

They both pulled out their knives and did as they were told.

'Where is Blue?' Steinberger asked.

'In the observation deck looking at the lab,' Kronch intoned.

'And the FZ-511 chopper? Where'd you land that?'

'On a helipad at the end of a small track behind the mansion,' the other goon answered.

'Keys?'

Kronch handed them over.

'Now.' Steinberger looked towards Suave. 'We have to wake him up.'

'I know how.' Max smiled broadly then looked at Kronch. 'Take off your sock.'

Kronch bent into the wriggling worm bath and after a few seconds held up a worn and muddied sock.

'That's a hard life for a sock.' Linden cringed.

'Hold it here.' Max pointed beneath Suave's nose.

'I know Suave has annoyed you,' Linden conceded, 'but does he really deserve this?'

After a few seconds, the agent spluttered to life. 'Wha—what is that . . . errr.'

'Suave,' Steinberger said in his calmest voice, 'we're in a room full of worms, but don't worry, we're about to escape and I need you to stay calm.'

Suave opened his eyes and had the same about-to-panic look as before. 'Did someone say worms? What's been happening?'

'We'll explain on the way.'

Max smirked. 'But for now it's probably best if you don't look down.'

Steinberger looked at the goons. 'Stay here,' he ordered, motioning to the others as he led the way out of the squirming bog.

Max was the last of the agents to squelch her way to worm freedom, but before she left she couldn't resist one last command. 'Why don't you two give yourselves a good slap?'

The goons slapped themselves across their cheeks.

Max giggled. This was fun. 'And . . . again?' They did as they were told.

'And now . . .'

'Max?' Linden's voice called.

'Coming.' She left the thugs in their rising worm compost, where she thought they looked right at home.

CHAPTER 19

SPY FORCE TO THE RESCUE!

In the damp and darkened corridor leading away from the giant compost room, Max, Linden, and Suave wiped off a few stray worms and began covering themselves in invisibility cream Steinberger had pulled from another pocket. Steinberger explained the rest of his plan.

'Max and Linden, you go to the roof and destroy the mind control device. Suave, once you're invisible, go to the distillery and get me a lab coat. There were some hanging just inside the door. That way I can masquerade as a scientist and save Frond.' He looked down at his Amazon-soaked, worm-slimed suit. 'And I may be a little noticeable dressed like this.'

'As good as done.' Suave was back to his normal Suave-self now they were worm free.

'Next, do you think you can fly Blue's helicopter?'

'The FZ-511? It'll be my pleasure, sir.'

'Excellent. Here are the keys. She's on a helipad at the end of a small track behind the mansion. We'll all meet you there in twenty minutes.'

'Will that be enough time?' Max asked as her legs and waist became invisible.

'It has to be,' Steinberger said sombrely. 'Once

Blue knows Frond has gone, there's no telling what he'll do.'

Max, Linden, and Suave applied the last of the cream to the visible parts of their bodies.

'Max and Linden, you'll need your super-grip gloves, so retrieve your bags from the bin outside the kitchen. Once you're on the roof, I'll send you a signal on your palm computers to destroy the mind control device with your lasers. But wait for my signal. I will need to keep Frond calm as she comes round and lead her out of the lab with the minimum of fuss.'

Steinberger gazed proudly at where his team would be if he could see them. 'I am prouder of you than any Spy Force mission leader has ever been.'

His eyes moistened with tears and as much as Max knew it was an important moment, it wasn't time for any crying.

'May the Force be with you,' she announced.

'May the Force be with you,' the others sang musketeer-style.

Suave opened the door to the corridor and quickly made his way to find a lab coat, while Max and Linden hurried to the bin and found their packs. They were smothered in soggy food and sauces. 'I should have guessed,' Max moaned. She had a habit of attracting rubbish while on missions.

They wiped the packs down as best they could and began to apply the invisibility cream to them, just as an aproned man came out of the kitchen and witnessed the disappearing bags. They rubbed the cream in faster and within seconds both had vanished.

Max and Linden held their breath, standing as still as they could, waiting to see what the man would do. He stared at the space where they were crouched.

Please go away, Max pleaded silently.

The man shook his head. 'I think I need a holiday,' he said before walking back into the kitchen.

'Now let's get out of here,' Linden breathed.

They sneaked past a group of suited men laughing to each other importantly, and made their way out of the front entrance.

'Feel that heat,' Max sighed quietly to Linden as the jungle temperature hit her.

'It's a scorcher, all right.'

It wasn't Linden who answered.

Max flung her head to the right to see a burly guard standing beside her. She held her breath, not knowing what to do.

'What?' a guard to the left side of them asked.

'Feel that heat. Isn't that what you said?'

'Wasn't me.'

Max and Linden stood frozen between the two guards, who looked suspiciously around.

'Must be getting to me.' The first guard wiped his brow as Max and Linden tiptoed past and made their way silently into the front yard.

Linden stopped. 'Max?'

'Ooph.' Max head-butted Linden's pack. 'Did you have to stop so suddenly?'

'I wanted to make sure you were there,' Linden whispered. 'And not back there making conversation with the guards.'

'Funny,' Max answered. 'Let's go round the corner where they won't hear us. And before you kill me with your hilarity.'

After putting invisibility cream on their super-grip gloves and slipping them on, they were about to start climbing when they were interrupted by something they'd forgotten.

'The dogs!' Linden stared at the two growling animals, circling them and sniffing the air. He ran to the corner of the mansion to see if the guards had noticed. 'We've got to quieten them down before the guards hear.'

'The Hypnotron?' Max suggested.

'Will it work on animals?'

'We're about to find out.'

Max took her Hypnotron out of her bag. The dogs whimpered at the small marble-sized device seemingly floating before them. With one small squeeze, a blast of golden light shot into their eyes.

Linden looked at the guards. They were talking to each other but stopped when they heard the dogs whining even louder. 'They're coming.'

'Quick,' Max pleaded to the device as the thirty seconds ticked closer.

The guards surveyed the area as they thudded towards the whining dogs.

'Twenty-seven, twenty-eight, twenty-nine . . .' Max counted.

'Thirty,' Linden whispered. 'Lie down.'

The dogs did as they were told. The guards came up and stood beside an invisible Max and Linden.

'What's up, fellas?'

Max and Linden barely breathed.

The guards looked around to see what had upset the dogs.

'Must have been a snake,' one suggested.

'Think they'd be used to them by now.'

'Are you?'

'Nope. Things give me the creeps. Let's get back.'

Max and Linden waited until the guards had turned the corner before they made their move. Max placed one hand on the wall. 'Here goes.' She then placed another and, taking a deep breath, hoisted herself up. 'Hey, these are great.'

Linden started climbing beside her. 'I bet this is how Spiderman felt when he first got his spider powers. You going to be OK with the height?'

Max smiled. 'Sure, all I have to do is not look down.'

'That's a great idea, I wish I'd thought of it.'

'Stick with me and you'll learn all sorts of things.'

They quickly made their way to the top of the roof and, finding the mind control device, contacted Steinberger. 'We're in place,' Max typed.

They pulled out their lasers and awaited their next instructions.

Having buttoned a lab coat over his damp and crumpled suit, Steinberger put on the pair of safety glasses that were in the pocket, pushed his hair under a hair net, and strode confidently down the mansion's elaborate corridors to the distillery and to the greatest moment of his life.

He felt proud. He felt brave.

But when he stepped inside the distillery, he felt petrified.

His breath shortened when he saw Frond. His hands shook and his brow dotted with the usual splatter of nervous sweat.

'May the Force be with you,' he whispered to himself as he patted down his coat and concentrated on walking over to her without falling down.

'Dr Frond, I just wanted to say what a pleasure it is to work with someone as talented as you.'

Frond looked up from the Spy Force manual and for a moment Steinberger thought he saw a glimmer of recognition in her eyes. 'Have we met before?'

Steinberger's heart faltered. He wanted to tell her it felt as if he'd known her all his life. 'Only briefly, during various group briefings.'

'Oh.' Frond was still curious.

Steinberger looked up and noticed Blue in the observation room with his back to the glass. He had to get Frond out of there before Blue turned around and saw them.

'I think the lab's work on the sleeping sickness formula was inspired. And now you're working on an elixir for life?'

'Yes. It will be fantastic. Excuse me for a moment.'

Steinberger melted. He would have thrown himself into a bubbling vat if she'd asked. He gazed at her as she moved to the steaming elixir nearby. Then something he saw on the bench made him snap out of it. A large collection of plant and animal samples.

Including a jar of triatoma bugs.

'The bugs,' he whispered.

As Frond measured another ingredient into her elixir, Steinberger discreetly took out his Mini Transporter Capsule and, feeling like a bank robber in broad daylight, placed a few bugs inside. He entered the Spy Force coordinates and pressed *send.* The bugs were on their way. He hoped it wasn't too late.

He then reached into his pocket for his palm computer. As Frond stirred her steaming creation, he pressed *send* again, this time on a pre-programmed message. Milliseconds later, Max and Linden got their call.

* * *

'It's Steinberger.' The two invisible spies jumped to their feet and held their lasers steady.

'All set?' Max was ready to enjoy every minute of destroying Blue's device.

'Definitely,' Linden replied.

'Fire.'

Two sharp red beams cut through the air and blasted into the heart of the mind control device. Melting steel and burning cables sizzled and cracked before them. A veil of bitter-smelling smoke stung their noses. Then, finally, the machine collapsed into itself like an ice-cream cake in the sun.

Linden wiped his brow with his sleeve. 'Some of my best work, I think.'

Max shrugged. 'I've seen you do better. Now let's get to the helicopter.'

The two spies packed their bags, crept to the edge of the roof and began their super-grip descent to the ground, with Max concentrating on each move and on not looking down.

Frond slumped against her workbench like a puppet whose strings had been suddenly cut. Steinberger swept in next to her and held her up. He had just seconds to get her out of there.

'Frond, it's me, Steinberger. You've been kept against your will by a mind control device in Blue's distillery in the Amazon jungle. I'm going to get you out of here and back to Spy Force.'

Frond was confused. 'I've been what?'

Steinberger smiled in relief. The real Frond would never be capable of agreeing to work with Blue.

'Have I done anything bad? I can't seem to remember what I've been doing.'

Steinberger touched her hands. 'You could never do anything bad.'

Steinberger was finally speaking to Frond without stumbling, but before he could say any more, he looked up and saw what he'd been dreading. Blue had seen them and was waving his hands and yelling into a phone.

'There's no time to explain. We have to go. Do you trust me?'

Frond paused momentarily before saying, 'Of course.'

Steinberger's heart leapt over itself. 'Let's go, then.'

Grabbing the Spy Force manual and slipping it under his lab coat, Steinberger asked Frond, 'Do you know a quick way out?'

'I don't even remember how I got here,' she answered sadly.

Steinberger smiled reassuringly. 'Looks like we'll have to find one together.'

They ran out of the distillery and down long and winding corridors, lined with elaborate chandeliers, busts of Blue on marble stands, and walls filled with portraits of him posing as a great explorer.

A piercing whistle shot over their heads. They turned to see two of Blue's guards aiming stun blasters at them.

'In here.' Steinberger grabbed Frond's hand and took her through a small door. They rushed past baskets of sheets and clothes, the noise of washing machines, and the steam of heat presses.

'Sorry.' Steinberger apologized after almost bowling over a weighty woman in a white uniform, but seconds later they heard her scream. The guards had pushed her aside into a basket of washing. Her legs fumbled through the air as the guards ran past her.

'Duck!' Steinberger shouted to Frond. They leapt behind a clothes rack, only barely missing being blasted.

Steinberger then noticed an exit through racks of starched lab coats. 'This way.'

They crawled along the ground while the guards angrily overturned baskets of laundry and pushed through racks of clothes in search of the two escapees.

Another shot from the stun blasters whistled past them. Steinberger saw a large fan and a barrel of soap powder and had an idea. 'Use this to cover your nose.' He handed Frond a folded and ironed handkerchief. He carefully pulled the fan so it faced into the barrel as the goons' search brought them closer and closer. He switched on the fan, filling the air with an irritating white soapy cloud. Hoping the dust from the powder would provide cover, Steinberger sprang towards the exit, removed the key, and opened it quickly. He then pulled Frond gently through and locked the door behind them as the goons fell into uncontrollable sneezing.

'That'll give us some time,' he predicted as he and Frond ran to the path at the back of the house that he hoped would lead to the helipad.

Frond's beehive hairdo flopped around her ears and Steinberger's shoes once again struggled with the uneven ground beneath them.

Minutes later they heard the crash of the laundry door breaking, followed by sneezing and the thud of heavy footsteps thundering after them.

But then they heard something else. The propeller blades of a chopper coming to life.

'This way,' he puffed excitedly, holding the Spy Force manual in one hand and Frond's hand in the other. After a few more hurried steps, the track ended abruptly at the helipad. The wind from the chopper blades was blasting overhead. Max and Linden, having applied the Invisibility Cream antidote, waved furiously as the agents ran towards them.

They also saw the guards.

'Quick,' Max called out. 'They're behind you.'

Suave had the controls poised for take-off. Steinberger reached the craft first and, with Max and Linden, helped Frond inside.

'Welcome back,' Linden beamed.

'Thank you,' Frond breathed.

A stun blast ricocheted off the side of the chopper as the burly goons sneezed and got ready to take another shot.

The chopper lifted slightly off the ground. Steinberger handed the Spy Force manual to Max and quickly hoisted himself inside. 'What about the triatoma?' Max remembered with a sickening jolt.

'They're travelling first class in a transporter capsule straight to Finch.'

Max's face softened beneath a wide smile. 'You're my hero, you know that.' Steinberger blushed a burning red.

Then Max saw Blue. He'd followed the guards and was running up behind them, puffing and panting. 'Stop them!' he shouted above the roaring blades, his face twisted into an ugly rage.

The helicopter lifted into the air as another shot barely missed Steinberger's head.

Max was furious.

She grabbed her Hypnotron and aimed it at Blue and his goons.

She then realized what she could do. If she wanted, now was her chance to lock Blue away for ever in a world of hypnosis. She stared at the man who had used and hurt Ben, Eleanor, and Francis, had kidnapped her father and even caused the death of Linden. She felt a rising fury in her chest. Getting revenge would feel so sweet.

But then she remembered Quimby's warning. If she hypnotized him for ever, it would make her just as bad as him. Max gritted her teeth and watched as Blue yelled at the thugs to shoot. They tried to take aim but their sneezing fits sent shots off into the jungle. Max set the Hypnotron for twenty minutes and blasted them for thirty seconds.

'Heel!' she yelled. The goons and Blue obeyed, squatting on the ground like obedient hounds. 'Chase your tails.'

She watched them turn circles on all fours and smiled.

The helicopter swung away from the mansion, higher and higher, leaving Blue, his mansion and his distillery well behind them.

CHAPTER 20

GOODS CARRIERS, HOSPITAL BEDS, AND PRISON CELLS

The Goliath was a large dome-shaped goods carrier that had responded immediately to Alex's call for assistance. Despite its bulky size, it had made its way effortlessly into the heart of the Amazon jungle. Using the locator on Sleek's palm computer, the Goliath crew pinpointed the Invisible Jet. As the FZ-511 chopper swerved into view, they were using powerful cranes to lift the jet from its tree-top position into the cargo hold.

'The Goliath,' Suave whispered reverently from the chopper's controls. Minutes later, he'd guided the FZ-511 into the Goliath's hold with faultless ease.

The crew of the Goliath welcomed them and directed them into the plush, air-conditioned interior. Sleek was still in the grip of the sleeping sickness and had been nestled carefully into a hospital bed and monitored by the crew's doctor.

The trip back to Spy Force was filled with an air of satisfied exhaustion. At least until the mention of food.

'Food?' Linden was ready to kiss the Goliath crew member handing him a menu. 'You've saved my life. Twice!'

As they ate, Max and Linden enjoyed Steinberger's stumbling and blushing as he explained to Frond all that had happened. After he'd finished, Frond's normally bright demeanour had become downcast.

'I'm sorry for all the trouble I've caused,' she apologized, sad and frightened at how easily her mind had been captured by Blue. 'I . . .' her voice cracked.

Steinberger steeled himself. 'It was an honour rescuing you.'

There was an awkward pause. Max and Linden shot each other wide smiles as they stared at a furiously blushing Frond and Steinberger. Maybe now Steinberger was finally going to say how he felt. They watched as his lips quivered, his brow moistened, his eyes flicked back and forth in their sockets. He opened his mouth, took a deep breath, and said, 'These cheese pastries are good, aren't they?'

There was a second's silence before Frond added, 'Yes. Very tasty.'

And the moment was gone, filled with the crunching sounds of cheesy pies as the conversation turned to safer topics the rest of the way back to Spy Force.

* * *

On the Goliath's arrival at the VART, the medical team were waiting to rush Sleek to the infirmary.

There was also someone else.

'Alex!' Max began to rush towards her but, realizing she may have looked a little too excited, slowed down and put her hands into her jungle- and worm-smeared pockets. 'Hi.'

Alex gave what could have been called a smile. 'Welcome back and well done on completing your mission.'

Max blushed. Alex had just congratulated her! She was happy to see her! She was . . .

'Max, I think it's time to stop staring now,' Linden whispered. 'I'm not having a spy partner who could double as a flycatcher.' He grinned.

Max closed her mouth and tried to look casual in searching for something else to look at.

As Sleek's hospital bed was wheeled off the Goliath, Alex filled them in on what had been happening. 'The triatoma bug arrived here just in time for Finch and his team to create the antidote. It's been administered to the sick agents. Most of them are still a bit hazy, but after a few days they'll all be back to normal.' Alex turned to Frond. 'Good to have you back. Finch will be very relieved to have you safely with us again.'

Frond smiled. 'I won't be going anywhere again soon, I promise.'

Alex looked at the bedraggled agents before her. 'Now that you're back, Finch has ordered full medical check-ups.' She looked around her. 'Where's Suave?'

Suave, who had been unusually quiet for the entire trip home, was nowhere to be seen.

'I'll make sure he reports to the infirmary.' Steinberger's mouth twisted into a frown. 'Alex?' he asked carefully. 'How's Harrison?'

'He's fine.' She paused. 'He's asked to see you.'

'Thought so.' Steinberger knew it was time to face the consequences of disobeying his chief's commands.

After being checked over by Finch in the infirmary, Max, Linden, and Steinberger were directed down a polished white corridor to the room where Harrison was recovering. As they entered, they could hardly see him for all the white-coated medical staff busily checking his temperature, feeling his pulse, and monitoring his heartbeat.

'Ah.' Harrison sat up as the agents stood in the doorway. 'I've been baking for you . . . Oh, blast.' He looked agitated. 'I mean, *waiting* for you.'

There was something in his tone that made Max and Linden feel uneasy.

The medical assistants heard it too. They finished their tasks and promptly left the room.

A loaded pause fell between them as Harrison stared at the newly arrived agents. Linden brushed a stray piece of hair from his forehead only for it to spring back again. Max could tell Harrison was going to reprimand Steinberger, but after all he'd been through, she just couldn't let him.

'Mr Harrison, sir, I know what Steinberger did wasn't exactly by the book or your word but you have to know that if it wasn't for him . . .'

'That'll do, Max,' Harrison said, with a finality that scared her. 'I know what you're going to spray . . . I mean, *say*.'

'You do?'

Harrison straightened out his bedcovers. 'Suave came by earlier and told me everything.'

'Everything?' Max was hoping he'd left a few parts out. Like her falling out of the tree and yelling at Suave for saving them.

'Yep. He would have been a good agent.' He paused. 'Once he'd got over his fear of worms.'

'Would have been?' Max frowned.

'Yes, I'm afraid despite anything I could say to

convince him otherwise, he's resigned from the Force.'

'Resigned?' Max said incredulously and a little guiltily. 'He can't resign.'

'I feel the same way.' He coughed and took a few seconds to get his breath.

'Max and Linden, your level of bravery never ceases to erase me . . . *amaze* me. I feel I don't say it enough but I want you to know that Spy Force is very proud to have you on our team.'

Linden sneaked Max a small victory smile but it was wiped away by what Harrison had to say next.

'As for you, Steinberger.'

Steinberger straightened up, preparing himself for what was about to come.

'You directly disobeyed orders, put your life in grave danger, and went into the field without any proper training. The possibilities for catastrophe were bendless . . .' Harrison winced. 'I mean, *endless*.'

Max stared at Harrison's stern, determined face.

'Yes, sir. I'm sorry, sir.'

Linden gulped.

Harrison shuffled in the starched infirmary sheets, looking as if he hated every minute of being a patient. 'As it happens, your being on that mission was crucial for its success. As such, Spy Force is deeply indebted to you and we're giving you a two-week holiday to any destination of your choice.'

Steinberger lifted his sagging head. 'Thank you, sir.'

'But let me say this: if you disobey Spy Force orders again, it won't be a holiday you will be getting.'

'Yes, sir. Of course, sir.'

Steinberger hung his head but Max noticed a small smile of quiet pride on his face. She knew that if he was ever faced with the same dilemma, he'd do it all over again.

'Sir?' Steinberger asked. 'What about Agent Dretch?'

'Yes. Dretch.' Max and Linden could read the guilt in Harrison's eyes over how Dretch had been treated. 'Release him immediately and tell him I'd like to see him,' he said gruffly. 'And make it quick, otherwise Finch's assistants are going to be back with all their flossing . . . that is, *fussing*.'

'Yes, sir.'

'And Steinberger?'

'Yes, sir?'

'Thank you for bringing Frond safely back to us.'

Steinberger's lips quivered. He went to reply but closed his mouth without saying anything.

'Sir?' Max asked. 'What will happen to Blue?'

'Alex organized for an international police team to travel on the Goliath to Blue's mansion so they could inspect his jungle projects. Luckily for us, you thought to hypnotize him, Max, because he's been questioned and taken into custody. Funny thing was, though, he kept breaking into intermittent barking.'

Max broke into a cheeky grin.

'Blue's been arrested?' For all his evil schemes, Max knew Blue always covered his tracks. It was hard to imagine he'd ever let himself be caught. 'That's great news!'

Harrison's face clouded over. 'I am worried, I must confess, that after all these years of anger towards the Force, we won't have seen the last of him. Or perhaps even the worst.'

Max swallowed. She still remembered the look of rage on Blue's face just before she hypnotized him.

A nurse bustled into the room, wriggled her way between the agents and the chief, and waved them out. 'That will do, I'm afraid. Mr Harrison is not to be tired out and I must ask you to leave.'

Harrison sighed as the bustling nurse took over and he was once again surrounded by a flurry of thermometers, white coats, and overly fussy activity.

The Spy Force cells were buried deep within the furthest and lowest layers of the Force. The terracotta elevator that took them there made various downwards and sidewards movements, until it slowed to a gentle whirr. Then stopped. Halfway between the two floors.

'At least with things back to normal we can concentrate on fixing these elevators.'

The agents crouched down and jumped out of the elevator into a long, grey, echoing passage that drabbed its way past a series of iron gates and bolted doors.

'He should be in number thirteen,' Steinberger whispered.

'Lucky,' Linden winced. They made their way past the other empty cells before coming to number thirteen.

Dretch lay on a narrow bed under a single

light bulb. Delilah was perched on the end keeping watch, and at the sight of the agents standing before her, she sent out a low, throaty growl.

Dretch sat up, took Delilah in his arms, and whispered a gentle *shhhh*. The CRISP guard on duty opened the gate and let them in. Steinberger stood before his friend, wringing his hands, explaining everything that had happened in small broken sentences.

He paused as he tried to work out how to say the next part. 'I never for a moment thought you . . .' but he stopped, knowing nothing he could say would express how sorry he was, or take back the time Dretch had innocently spent in the cells.

Dretch ran his fingers down Delilah's fur. His small and crooked body looked even smaller in his crumpled maroon coat. He'd never been a man who depended much on words. He tucked both hands deeply into his pockets and said nothing. Steinberger's heart heaved in fear at the possibility of losing a dear friend.

Max looked closely at Dretch's face and thought she saw the beginnings of a tear form beneath his spaghetti fringe.

'You did what you needed to do. Loyalty to the Force must come first.'

He said nothing more, and the smile on Steinberger's face told Max and Linden he didn't need to.

'Is there anywhere you'd like to go?' Steinberger asked.

'How's Irene?'

'You know Irene. Soon after she'd had the antidote, she was back in the kitchen. She's not a hundred per cent yet but I'm sure she will be soon.'

'Is the kitchen open?' Dretch, like most agents in the Force, had a real passion for Irene's food.

Steinberger laughed. 'I believe it's been given the all clear.'

'Yeah, well, what are we standing around here for?' Dretch complained as he moodily walked past the agents. 'I've got better things to do than . . .' His mumbling continued as he walked down the corridor towards the elevators.

'Looks like Dretch is back to his old cheery self,' Max smiled.

'Yeah,' Linden smirked. 'I don't think you've got anything to worry about there, Steinberger.'

'Well? What are you all waiting for? You want

me to carry you there?' Dretch had reached the elevator.

'I think you're right.' Steinberger sighed happily and they all hurried to scramble up into the elevator for a one-way trip straight to Irene's kitchen.

'I think I ate too much.' Even though Linden had been transported through space and time, escaped the clutches of a nightmare vortex, and ridden in some of the world's most advanced vehicles, Irene's food was still the one thing that could send him into a sigh-filled, brain-frozen daze.

Despite Finch's orders for Irene to have complete bedrest for at least another twenty-four hours, Linden knew there'd be nothing that could keep her away from doing what she did best.

'If you decide you could fit more in, there's plenty left.' She ruffled his hair and spoke to Dretch and Max.

'I missed you, Irene.' Linden stared at the colourful woman sitting beside him as her hand rested on his shoulder. 'I don't know what I'd do if you hadn't recovered.'

His voice strained and cracked.

Irene's eyes filled with tears. 'You're one special munchkin, aren't you?' She pulled Linden into her full arms and colourful layers for a hug.

After a few moments, she wiped her eyes. 'Now, off you all go. I've got plenty of recovering agents to feed, thanks to you lot.'

Max and Linden stood up from their canteen chairs.

'Thanks, Irene. For everything,' Max said before they both threw themselves at Irene for a final hug.

'Oh, now that's got the old waterworks going.'

Max and Linden moved away smiling as Irene wiped her handkerchief across her eyes. 'I'll have something even more special when I see you next time.' Tears welled up again, blurring everything around her. 'Now go on, you've got a home to go to, haven't you?'

They gave her one more smile before turning to leave.

But there was one last person Max needed to say goodbye to.

'Bye, Dretch. It's nice to know such a good agent.'

Dretch grumbled and Max took it as a thankyou before they ran from the canteen.

Dretch stared at his plate as Irene turned back to the kitchen, a small, almost imperceptible smile hanging on his lips.

'Yeah. Thanks, kid.'

Linden followed Max and Steinberger as they walked down the long metal walkway of the VART. As they entered the giant vehicle hangar, they saw a figure slumped in a chair sitting before an empty space.

'Sleek?' Steinberger asked softly.

There was no answer. The Invisible Jet had been very badly damaged and Sleek, who had left the infirmary against Finch's advice, was simply staring at her. Sleek's skills with people ranged from awkward to cold, but his affection for the vehicles in the VART was like the closest of friendships.

'Will she be OK?' Max asked.

Sleek slowly lifted his hands, pointed randomly then lowered them again, lost for where to begin.

Linden walked over to him and offered his hand. 'Thanks, Sleek. For everything.'

Sleek looked up, coughed, and awkwardly held out his hand.

'It was a pleasure working with you,' Linden said.

Sleek looked as if he wanted to say something, but instead turned and kept staring at his broken jet.

Max, Linden, and Steinberger walked to the centre of the VART.

'He'll have it back to full operation in no time,' Steinberger assured them. 'He's repaired vehicles that have been returned in more pieces than went into building them.'

'Max. Linden.'

It was Suave. Not the confident Mr Do-No-Wrong of before, but a more subdued version.

'I wanted to see you before you left, to thank you for all you did on the mission. It was a real privilege working with you.' He looked at Steinberger. 'Even though I may not have seemed to have appreciated all your skills.'

'You make a brilliant agent, Suave,' Steinberger assured him.

Suave looked awkward. 'Except for an obvious fear of . . .' He couldn't bring himself to say it. 'I'm sorry I let you all down.' He paused. 'Can I talk to you, Max? In private?'

Steinberger and Linden moved away. 'We'll be over here.'

Max was silent. Sure, Suave was a little out of action when the worms appeared, but other than that he was perfect. 'Suave, Harrison told us you've resigned.' The agent nodded sadly. Max frowned. 'But you can't. You're a great agent. You landed us in the Amazon when Sleek passed out, were able to drive every vehicle we came across, and got us back to Spy Force. That's not what I call letting us down.'

Even though Max had thought Suave had been a major pain, she was surprised to realize she actually meant what she'd just said.

'Thanks.' Suave looked as if there was something else he needed to say. 'You were right to be suspicious when we first met in the VART. I *was* staring at you, but it was because I'd heard so much about you. About how young you are, how you always solve all your missions, and how you have this wild and unique way of doing it.'

Max suddenly felt very self-conscious.

'I guess I just envied you,' Suave continued.

'Me?' Max looked around to see if he was talking to someone else.

'And there's something else.' Suave took a deep breath. 'I knew Sleek had eaten the muffin.'

Max's eyes opened wider.

'When Steinberger and I found Sleek passed out in the jet, I saw the half-eaten muffin on the floor. I quickly picked it up and put it in my bag before Steinberger could see.'

'But why—'

'Because it was my first mission and I wanted to do everything perfectly. And because I wanted you to think I was a good agent.'

Max couldn't believe what she was hearing. Suave was a brilliant agent and here he was thinking he wasn't good enough!

'You messed up once. We all do that. In fact now that we've been on a mission together you'll know with me it's a few more times than once.'

Suave made a weak attempt to smile.

'I can't wait until the next time we work together,' she said.

'You mean it?'

'Sure.' Max smiled. 'Only maybe next time, somewhere with a few less plane crashes and worms.'

Suave shivered. 'Definitely.'

Max looked up into his eyes. 'Please don't resign.'

Suave looked towards the exit, then back at Max. 'You mean that?'

'I have this terrible habit of meaning what I say.'

Suave smiled. 'I'll think about it.'

'Good.'

Steinberger walked over and was pleased to see the two agents smiling. 'Max, you and Linden had better go. I've spoken to Ben and Eleanor and they are very keen to have you back.'

Max stared at the Steinberger who had been transformed from talkative Administration Manager to a self-assured man of action. She'd never felt it before, but this time it was hard to say goodbye.

'Max? Is something wrong?' Steinberger was worried she might be getting sick.

Max knew if she answered she'd probably turn into a blubbering cry-baby. She threw her arms around his waist and hoped that would say it all.

When she let go, Steinberger's eyes were rimmed with tears. 'Thank you, Max.'

Linden entered the details of their destination into the Time and Space Machine. Address: Mindawarra, Australia. He patted his full stomach. 'Hope the machine is going to handle the extra weight.'

Then Linden thought, 'Wonder if Ben's saved me some of that lasagne?' Max laughed.

'What?' Linden feigned shock. 'Bye, Steinberger. See you on the next mission, eh?'

'I think that was enough in-field experience for one lifetime.' Steinberger had never pictured himself as an in-field agent, but now he'd done it, he felt quietly pleased.

Max and Linden watched as Steinberger and Suave moved away, noticing a spring-filled step and an overall togetherness in Steinberger that they'd never seen in him before.

'He'll go on another mission,' Linden predicted. 'I guarantee it!'

'Yeah, but do you think he'll tell Frond he likes her?' Max asked.

'Leading dangerous Spy Force missions is one thing,' Linden smirked. 'Telling Frond he likes her might need a few more years to work up to.' He frowned. 'Speaking of telling . . . what were you going to tell me at the waterfall?'

'Sorry?' Max did a terrible job of trying to look confused.

'You wanted to say something as we headed for the waterfall.'

Max tried to think of something to get her out of this. At the waterfall she had thought they were going to die. It had seemed like a good idea to tell

Linden how she felt about him, but now that they were safe, it seemed like the worst idea she'd ever had.

'We should go.' And before Linden could object, Max said 'transport' and they were flung through space away from Spy Force towards a small farm in Mindawarra, Australia.

A cold night one month later . . .

The sound of metal clanging against metal tore into his head like a migraine. His hands flew to cover his ears as he delved down deeper into the prickly prison-issue blanket. Grey filtered light seeped into his cell like a cold drizzling chill. Outside, freedom sat like a piece of rich chocolate cake. Tantalizing and out of reach.

Blue looked at the blackened, moon-smudged sky through his cell bars and groaned.

He pulled his knees closer to his chest for warmth, the thin prison-issue uniform doing nothing to drive away the cold.

His fury and discomfort would make it hours before he'd be able to sleep, and until then, he only muttered one thing.

'Next time.'

When Deborah Abela was a small child, she spent most of her time imagining she was on great adventures all over the world. When she grew older, she bought a backpack and a plane ticket and actually went on them. After three years she came home and worked for seven years on one of Australia's most popular children's TV programmes, before leaving to write novels about a small girl who goes on lots of adventures all over the world.

Deborah grew up in Merrylands, a western suburb of Sydney, but now lives in inner-city Glebe with her partner Todd, who is almost as nice as Linden.

ALEX CRANE, SUPER SPY, HAS ONLY MINUTES TO SAVE THE WORLD FROM TOTAL DESTRUCTION . . .

Max Remy, on the other hand, has the whole summer to get through with her crackpot aunt and uncle and weirdo Linden. Then Max discovers that her uncle is a brilliant scientist, on the brink of inventing a machine that can transport people through time and space.

Can she and Linden use the machine to find her long-lost relative in England? And if they do, will they be a match for the evil Mr Blue who wants to drown the kids in a giant green jelly?

Alex Crane could do it, so surely it will be a piece of cake for Max and Linden?

ISBN-13: 978-0-19-275418-9

ISBN-10: 0-19-275418-1

'DON'T YOU THINK WE SHOULD WORK OUT A PLAN BEFORE WE SNEAK UP ON ONE OF THE MOST CRIMINAL MASTERMINDS IN THE WORLD?'

A good idea—if only there were time!
The evil Mr Blue has cooked up a concoction that, when eaten, will control the minds of children the world over. And he's about to start acting on his half-baked plan.

Can super spies Max and Linden foil the plot? Will they see that Blue gets his just desserts? Or will their fiendish foe finally have his cake *and* eat it?

ISBN-13: 978-0-19-275419-6
ISBN-10: 0-19-275419-X

'NOW, IF YOU'LL EXCUSE ME, I MUST GO AND SUPERVISE THE END OF SPY AGENCIES THE WORLD OVER . . .'

Evil Mr Blue is back. And this time he's wriggled his reptilian way right into the heart of the Academy of Spies. The world's greatest spy agency is holding its annual awards dinner, which means that the world's greatest spies are all in one place.

Also in that place is a huge dormant volcano. And Blue's managed to wake it up. If Max, Linden and Ella can't calm things down, the whole thing's going to go sky high.

Will their super spy training help them save the day? Or will Max's fear of heights spell the end for Spy Force . . .

ISBN-13: 978-0-19-275420-2

ISBN-10: 0-19-275420-3

'BIGGUS FARTIE IS ONE OF OUR BEST SCIENTISTS. I WANT YOU TO SAVE HIM BEFORE A FOUL-SMELLING PLAN IS LET LOOSE ON THE WORLD.'

Lights! Camera! Action! Max and Linden are on a Spy Force mission in Hollywood–but it's not all films and fun.

Somebody has kidnapped Dr Fartie and is forcing him to encrypt movies. Now, top-secret security information is being passed to baddies the world over. Worse, it looks as if someone Max knows has infiltrated Spy Force.

Who can the pair trust? How will they find Fartie? And will Max's bad mood finally lead to somebody's sticky end?

ISBN-13: 978-0-19-275421-9

ISBN-10: 0-19-275421-1